Storyhouse

A BLANKET
OF EMBERS

Andy Kind

McKnight
&Bishop
Ltd

ABOUT THE PUBLISHER

McKnight & Bishop are always on the lookout for new authors and ideas for new books. If you write or if you have an idea for a book, please email:

info@mcknightbishop.com

Some things we love are undiscovered authors, open-source software, Creative Commons, crowd-funding, Amazon/Kindle, faith, social networking, laughter and new ideas.

Visit us at **www.mcknightbishop.com**

Copyright © Chris Bomford 2023

The rights of Andy Kind to be identified as the Author of this Work has been asserted by him in accordance with Section 77 of the Copyright, Designs and Patents Act 1988.

ISBN 978-1-905691-78-4

A CIP catalogue record for this book is available from the British Library.

First published in 2023 by McKnight & Bishop Inspire, an imprint of:
McKnight & Bishop Ltd
35 Limetree Avenue, Kiveton Park, South Yorkshire, S26 5NY
http://www.mcknightbishop.com | info@mcknightbishop.com

This book has been typeset in **Brandon Grotesque**, Garamond & Gotham Thin

CONTENTS

*For Lydia, who syringed out the despair
and bandaged me up with hope
- like any good nurse.*

All the very best, LP, and Amen xx.

INTRODUCTION

Who has time to read a novel these days? Without having done any kind of research, I can brazenly assert that the answer is 'nobody'. Short stories are the way forward, and so I've written some on the pages that follow.

The stories range in style and tone and agenda, and so I've grouped them loosely into three categories: Night (the darker, bleaker tales), Dawn (the lighter, more redemptive ones), and Dusk (those on the liminal borders). All of them are 'pandemic babies', the love-children of lockdown boredom and residual hopefulness. Writing was my major weapon for fighting off the doubt and despair that probably came knocking at most of our doors during Covid, and writing short stories offered me an escape from four lonely walls and set the finishing line closer than a novel would have done. Sometimes you just need a quick win, don't you?

Which doesn't make it easy to write or finish anything. Although my comedy stand-up routines tend to be, essentially, performed short stories, having a live, on-stage persona makes them easier to craft and to tell: it's obvious who the narrator is and the audience has plenty of audio/visual clues which help guide their response. Writing for the page is different. How do you show rather than tell when your only tools are twenty six letters grouped in various assortments? How do you tell an earnest story when the author and the narrator aren't the same person and might not agree? That's been the challenge. The hardest part of penning any story is not working out what happens, but 'Who is it happening to?'

It's been said that all writing is wish-fulfilment. I think that can be true, but I also think that the realisation of nightmares (which is the opposite to wish fulfilment) can play a major role. For my part, with each tale I simply started with 'What if?' Some of the supposings are based on experiences from my own life: what if I had acted differently, or sooner; what if that person had chosen self-sacrifice over self-preservation? But that certainly doesn't mean that any of these stories are thinly veiled diary entries. Of the fictions contained herein, 'That Sunday' is the nearest thing to autobiographical reportage, while 'Nothing Like Redemption' feels the closest to home emotionally.

The freedom in writing fiction, though, is being able to borrow binoculars and step inside someone else's head without making moralistic judgements about them. I think that's a vital part of human interaction which most of us fail at anyway: how do you render someone's earnest intentions without projecting your own prediction or predilection? 'What if the narrator agreed with me as the author?' is not fiction; it's propaganda.

I'm interested in redemption and resurrection and reconciliation. I think the best stories, ultimately, are those in which the 3 R's win out in the end. But there are real-life stories, aren't there, where death and pride and brokenness seem to dominate. Telling and living those stories is hard, but as a favourite book of mine says somewhere, 'We do not hope for what we already have'.

Thank you for choosing Storyhouse 1.1. We hope it will give you minute after minute of pleasure.

Here, then…

Part 1:
DUSK

one

ILL-SUITED

(Long-listed for the Oxford Flash Fiction prize)

I should have had breakfast before I put my suit on really, but I'd hardly slept and I was desperate for my future life to start - as though donning full regalia ahead of schedule could somehow chivvy time along. Now I was dressed it just gave me more time to think about what was coming; what was unseen but definitely on its way.

We sat around the kitchen table at different stages of life and undress - me, Mark the Best Man, my nephew the Groomsman, Dad - all of us gripped in some way by that pleasant nausea that saves itself for wedding days and rollercoasters. Dad drummed stoical fingers on the pine tabletop while I slurped my coffee loudly - anything to disrupt the tense silences that settled when our collective thoughts synchronised on what lay ahead. Then Mark, still enslaved by last night's *Drambuie* or jittery about his Best Man's speech or both, stumbled over my foot and managed to confetti my *Moss Bros* jacket with a cartoonishly-stacked plate of greasy bacon and attendant condiments.

'It's fine, it'll be fine,' he assured me as he pawed at me frantically with paper towel, contracting the grease to a long-term tenancy of the jacket's inner fibres.

'Sorry,' he said, a beaten man. I outnumbered his five-letter apology with a gang of four-letter words. He picked up the floored bacon and, already shamed beyond hope of reprieve, ate it.

Without my jacket, the underlying gold waistcoat I'd picked out for its gold waistcoatiness seemed lurid and garish, and gave me the look of a festive butler.

'Wear my jacket, son,' Dad said. 'It's a warm day, I'm happy without.'

A good plan, if only Dad's blazer hadn't been tailored to fit him, and if only he wasn't several inches taller and waistier than me. I slipped the jacket on, or rather I slipped down into it, like a heavy toddler on a water slide.

'It makes me think of drowning,' my nephew said sadly.

'It looks like a wizard cursed you,' Mark added.

'You look like a little boy in his Dad's jacket.'

But it would have to do. Everyone else's jackets were far too small for me, and I'd look like Dr. David Banner had lost his temper at a corporate bash.

'You'll grow into it, scarecrow,' Dad said with a steady smile, the same words he'd used when he watched my first school blazer hang off me all those years ago. My wedding suit was exactly the same shade of royal blue - I hadn't realised, and smiled detachedly at the memory.

'Don't worry, you'll grow into it.'

The church was cool in the gathering summer heat, or maybe it was just the draughtiness of my jacket that kept my temperature down. The guests filtered in, everyone smiling politely, nobody referencing - at least not to me - the cavernous blazer that could have smuggled both me and several bibles into communist China. Mark sat still next to me, chewing anxiously on something that might have been gum or a rasher of pig he'd found under a pew.

Dad appeared at the back of church, sweat patches visible on his exposed shirt from where he'd pushed Mum's wheelchair up the church drive. He glided her chair down the aisle, humming or singing something just for her on a day that no bookie would have given odds on her seeing. I turned moistening eyes to the floor at that twenty-year-old memory of sitting in a sickly waiting room, being told along with my two sisters that Mum wasn't expected to last the week. They'd only been married seven years when it happened. Dad had sat with us in that room, the same age as I was today, as his colleagues told him what he already knew but was powerless against - a well-respected doctor sitting as helpless as a drowning boy, unable to heal his broken bride.

But healing is a process, not an event, and he did heal her; had gone on healing her for the next two decades. The general practitioner had hung up his stethoscope and become a specialist carer. To say I never heard him complain would be rose-tinted. The house, the one we downsized to, wasn't always a fun place to be. He shouted and swore and smashed things. I never saw him cry but I heard him.

He never left, though. Long after Eros had flown, Agape rolled up its sleeves and just got on with it.

Was she still beautiful to him? Did he recognise the woman he'd promised to love through sickness and poverty? Could he ever have guessed how quickly those promises would be tested? He set the brake on Mum's wheelchair and stood beside her. He was still humming something.

The vicar asked all those who could to stand. Mark roused himself and swallowed whatever had been incarcerated in his mouth. A hush poured into the church from the open arch doorway and the bridesmaids made their staggered procession to the front. Then came my bride.

My future stepped down the aisle towards me, clothed in perfect unblemished white.

I stood there waiting, drumming my fingers on my leg, in a coat that was far too big for me.

two

EARLY STAGES

Do you remember when I took you to London, my boy?

I t was your 6th birthday and you were desperate to go and see Buckingham Palace. I think you must have studied it at school or seen a picture in a book, but either way you were obsessed with seeing where the Queen lived, absolutely obsessed. So I booked us a couple of day-return tickets, and I must have been feeling pretty generous because usually I would have made sandwiches, but I remember on this occasion I said we could go to a restaurant and you liked the idea of going to a restaurant, so that's what we decided.

And we came out of Marylebone station and the first thing you said was, 'Mummy, London really smells!' And I said something like, 'Yes, welcome to the capital!' And I remember you looked quite frightened, with all those people and the high buildings, because even though you'd seen television programmes featuring London, it's not really the same, and I think you probably felt quite overwhelmed by it all. And as we went to cross the road I said, 'Take my hand,' and you said - I remember - 'No, Mummy, I'm a big boy and I don't need to hold your hand.' And you gave me a high-five, sort of in celebration of how grown up you thought you were, but also I think to swat me away!

And we took the tube to Charing Cross, didn't we? And you were ever so excited about being on a train that went under the ground.

I think that's one of the lovely things about children - they see things that grown ups have forgotten and they point them out, don't they? Well anyway, I thought Charing Cross would be a good station to choose because I could show you Trafalgar Square, and then we could walk down the Mall with Buckingham Palace appearing on the horizon. But of course life is never that simple, and you were complaining about how far you were having to walk - and we'd only recently arrived. I thought, oh gosh, this is going to be a long day, isn't it?

But you were very excited when you saw Buckingham Palace, I remember. You had with you one of those disposable cameras that I had bought you, a Kodak type of thing, because I thought you'd enjoy taking your own photos but I didn't want to have something stolen which was expensive, and you know what big cities can be like - well, of course you do, you live in one now. Well, you took about 20 photos from pretty much the same angle, using up all your film. We probably still have the photos somewhere, safe in the loft for posterity - or dinner for moths, more likely!

Then, when we'd only been there about five minutes, you said, 'Mummy, it's just a building.' And it's funny, isn't it, that you were much more awestruck by the underground trains than by the most famous building in the world. But I told you some of the history of the place, and I asked whether you thought the Queen was in and what she might be doing today. And you thought - I remember - you said, 'I think she's playing water polo'. And I don't have any idea why you said that - maybe you'd seen a poster or something - but I really did laugh at the idea of Her Majesty playing water polo, and the way you said it was so earnest, as though you really did think that might be happening.

But then you were bored. After all that, the thing we had come to see and you'd been obsessed with getting a glimpse of, well you'd had enough of that. So we found a playground nearby and I pushed you on the swings and you went down the slides. And then we found somewhere for lunch - I think it was called *Starburger*. But you wouldn't let me sit next to you, I had to sit opposite you because, you said, 'That's what big people do, Mummy, and I'm a big boy, remember? Remember, Mummy!' And you wagged your finger at me. And this big boy refused to order from the children's menu because you'd seen a picture of one of the special burgers and you wanted that, even after the waitress looked a bit sceptical at me. So you had it, and it came with onion rings and too much cheese, and I don't think you'd ever tried Barbecue sauce but it came with that. And after all that you didn't like it! 'It's too spicy, Mummy,' I remember you said. So I had two burgers, or as much as I could, and you just had your milkshake and some chips. And then ice-cream for afterwards, of course - even after the milkshake! It's a wonder you weren't sick.

So then I had the whole afternoon planned out. We were going to walk along the river and see the Houses of Parliament, and I had a voucher for Madame Tussauds which I thought we could use. But I could tell by the way you were walking - what I used to call your drunken sailor walk - that you just wanted to go home. And so I gave you the options: 'We can go to Madame Tussauds and see all the waxworks, or we can go and see Covent Garden, you know, with all the street performers…or we can just get the train and head back.' And at this your eyes flickered and widened, and I could tell that's what you wanted to do. You didn't want me to think you weren't enjoying yourself, but it was fine because we'd seen the thing we came to see, and London is a lot for children.

So we had a little walk along the river to Embankment and then we were going to catch the train back over to Marylebone. But it was a Saturday, and it was just after lunch, and of course all the football crowds were on their way to their different matches. This was before you really got into football. So we stood on the underground platform, and this big group of men came bustling along, singing and chanting about their football teams - not aggressively, they weren't doing anything wrong, but it was a lot of grown up men and they were quite boisterous. And I looked down at you and I could see you were frightened because, again, that was another new thing for you. So I said to you, 'Ooh, they're a bit scary, aren't they?' And you looked up at me, and you could see I was smiling and I wasn't really frightened, but you sort of stood on your tiptoes and said in your biggest voice, 'Don't be scared, Mummy. Hold my hand and I'll look after you.'

'Will my big boy look after me?' I said, and you nodded your head and said, 'Yes, I'll look after you, Mummy, don't worry.'

So I took your hand and gave your fingers a little squeeze, and we waited for the train to take us home. It had been such a nice day, and I remember it so well.

I just wanted you to know that story. And I want you to remember it because I'm frightened again - properly, this time. And if it gets to the point where I don't know who you are, I want you to tell me that story. I want you to take my hand and tell me that story. Tell me all about being pushed on the swings and the Queen playing water polo. And even if I don't recognise you, or I get confused, I want you to know that you will always have permission to hold my hand, my boy. Remember, will you?

three

THE REAL MARTHA MORRIS?

'm sitting on a marble balcony with a fantastic view out to the Mediterranean sea, enjoying a vodka martini like James Bond (thinking about having several more, like James Bond after a marriage breakup) and remembering the time I sent Martha Morris a private *Instagram* message to say: 'I think you've been cloned'. Some twopenny fraudster had duplicated her Instagram profile pic, lifted her entire bio and set up MarthaMorris978. That imposter had then messaged me saying, 'How are you, sir?'

My account clearly had my name as 'Joanne Gaskell', so whoever this low-level criminal was, they were rubbish at this. How are you, sir? SIR?! I mean, really.

'Thanks babes,' the real Martha responded. 'I don't know why people do this. It's not like I'm famous or important.'

'Maybe they just think you have an honest face or look like you've got gullible friends?' I replied. 'Honestly though, it's ridiculous what people do to make money.'

'Thanks for looking out for me, babes.'

'Anytime hun. I got you 😊Xxx.'

'It'll be great when this lockdown is over and we can meet in person 🎉.'

'Squeeeee!!! Literally I can't wait! Although how do I know this is the real Martha?! 🤔.'

'Erm....'

'Imagine if I turned up and you were this hulking brute who wanted to molest me.'

'Yes...imagine. Scary 😱.'

'Totally.'

'Jo, I promise I will never molest you.'

'Haha, thanks baby girl. They should put that in wedding vows. Night xx'

'Night, hun 😴.'

Between you and me, I despise text speak and emojis, but you get used to it when you spend enough time online.

Within a couple of days MarthaMorris978 had been removed from Instagram and there was just a 'User not available' box where the fake Martha had asked how I was, sir. The thing to look out for with these fake accounts is how they almost always use risible English or weird, archaic language. I got cloned once and a friend screenshotted me the message that FakeMe had sent to her. It said something bizarre like: 'Felicitations dear, I hope you're well and you look good on your photo methinks.' To be clear, I'm from twenty-first century Birmingham and have never been, much to my own chagrin, an extra from a Charles Dickens book - and my friend knew that incredibly well.

On another occasion I was messaged by a different friend who sounded linguistically authentic and tonally genial, which would have been convincing if I hadn't recently returned from his funeral. The money he went on to ask for seemed somewhat incongruous given he no longer had a working heart, let alone an active bank account.

The real Martha Morris was a separated mother of two who lived in Harpenden and, to quote her Instagram profile 'loves red wine, poetry and Ryan Gosling.' That's how we met, you see. My bio stated something similar: 'Location - Harpenden; loves books, el vino and all things Ryan Gosling'. I had posted a heftily hashtagged pre-lockdown selfie with 'The Gos' outside a London theatre, and Martha had written 'Jealous!!' in the comments, having been pulled there by the hook #RyanGoslingismyfuturehusband. I hearted her response and replied with a 😜; she followed me and I followed her straight back and thus began our story - as easy as that.

The balkanisation of real-life communities caused by the Covid-19 pandemic not only locked people indoors but dragged them online, desperate for a semblance of togetherness and connection. Human beings were reduced to avatars, but it was as close to real as they could make it. Women who couldn't meet friends for coffee bonded with strangers over celebrity crushes, and that's how Martha and I became friends. We shared stories of raising kids without a father; laughed maniacally over our descriptions of Swindon as being what would happen if Bristol was sick and London had diarrhoea and the twain met; debated heatedly over the best Gosling films and hair. It all came so easily.

The first time I thought Martha was deep-scamming me came in June. Her ex was apparently taking her to court over child access and 'What with the pandemic and not being able to get to work properly, I've got nothing to use.' I thought it would be a good idea to offer some financial support, 'Just the little that I can afford', but she was scandalised by the request and very apologetic because 'I never would ask you for money, babe, you don't even know me, although you're more like family than my family tbf.'

'You too chick, you know I'm here for you BFF,' I reassured her.

And she kept going on about how great it would be when we could finally meet, and I'd send gif after gif of moronic dances and celebrities downing cocktails on shows I'd never seen.

The second time I thought she was catfishing me, she got in touch all in capitals to say that her great-aunt who she barely knew had died and she'd inherited about £15,000. I shovelled out the OMG emojis and she riposted with a meme of a gangsta rapper throwing money everywhere in an irresponsible manner. But then eventually she stopped talking about it, and she kept saying how much she was looking forward to hooking up when lockdown was over, and I said: 'I'll be round with the wine and The Notebook as soon things open up.' I really liked her. Maybe it was the constant isolation of lockdown which affected my emotions differently, but these feelings weren't something to which I was accustomed.

Then I went quiet for a few days. It took her no more than an afternoon to work out something was wrong - that's how regular, how intimate, our contact had become.

'Seriously babes, what's going on?'

'I'm OK, just struggling with stuff at the mo,' I replied 48 hours later.

'Call me if you like, hun, I'm here for you anytime day or night.'

'Thanks love, I appreciate that x.'

Just after midnight on the third day of minimal contact, she messaged me again: 'Seriously JoJo, I'm so worried about you, you know you can talk to me.'

'HMRC have rejected my small business grant,' I lied, adding a cluster of 😫's and a 😩. I had informed Martha that I was a specialist house cleaner and, naturally, social distancing had put a lock on all that. 'I got the first grant no probs but they're now claiming I'm not eligible. It'll be OK, I'm just stressed.'

'Oh babes, I'm so sorry 💩,' she said.

'Don't worry. When I marry the Gos he'll sort all the money stuff out! 😋'

Always good to misdirect someone with a bit of humour.

'Babes seriously, give me your bank details and I'm putting money into your account rite now!'

'No, don't be silly, you can't do that.'

'I can and I will. I just got £15K from a dead relative - I'm a millionaire!'

'Did you legit get that money from your great aunt?' I asked, still hugely sceptical.

'Yes it was for realsies, now don't be such a silly cow, you can pay me back or whatevs when they sort your money - BANK DETAILS NOWWW!!!'

I gave her my bank details and she deposited £2,000 sterling into my account. I couldn't believe it - it was like an inverted heist.

'Let me know when it's in,' she said below a gif of playgirls in a jacuzzi.

'Yep, received. So nice!'

'You sorted now, hun??' Martha messaged the next day. And then…. 'Jo, u ok? 😊'

Surely, the 'User not available' message will have caused the penny to drop by now.

As I was saying earlier, it really is quite ridiculous what some people do to make money: working in jobs they don't want and pretending to enjoy them. If you're going to pretend to be someone you're not, do it on your own terms. And do it well.

'Another vodka martini?' the waiter enquires as I look out onto the glistening Mediterranean.

'Yes, please.' I close my laptop with a self-celebratory sigh.

'Are you well, sir?' the waiter asks.

'Yes…perfectly chipper, thank you. It's been a good day at work. I'll order the lobster later, methinks.'

'A very good choice, sir.'

four

A SWIFT 'ARF

East End of London, sometime in the early 1970s.

The Stag Inn was dingy, dirty and dire. But all that is gold does not glitter so they say and there was apparently a load of money stashed somewhere in there, hiding out behind regency tiles or stuffed inside rotten timbers. Either way, the rumour was out and the truth of it was now irrelevant. Chancers don't need facts; only chances.

Lucy the barmaid saw the wash of navy blue from behind the opaque window seconds before Bill entered.

'What can I get you, officer?' she said with staged deference. She looked well pretty in her barmaid's outfit.

'Just an apple juice, young lady, if you'd be so kind,' Bill replied, his officious manner failing to completely drown out the ring of Bow Bells in his voice.

'Coming right up!'

Lucy searched around furtively for a bottle of *Britvic* while the officer leant his uniformed arm on the counter's solid mahogany.

'You must be new,' Bill smirked, tapping a *Silk Cut* on the bar like a gavel.

'Been here about a couple of weeks, yeah,' the barmaid replied. 'Had a bit of bother down on the south coast if you catch my drift. Friend of my uncle's runs this place and said I could work a few shifts until I get myself sorted out.'

Bill's heavy eyes searched hers for hidden meaning. 'You've worked bars before though?'

'Yeah, yeah, since before I was legal.'

'Naughty girl.'

'Hey, I'm a good girl!' she protested from under the counter and under her eyebrows. They both allowed themselves a private smile.

'First time I've seen you in here though, officer,' Lucy said, reappearing, delving a hand into a plastic crate and pulling out...an orange juice.

'Been brought in specially, darlin',' Bill confided. 'There's a local firm knocking off businesses between Ilford and Bow and I'm here to bolster the ranks so to speak.'

'Oh yeah?' Lucy finally opened an orange juice and poured it into a wine glass.

'Yeah...,' Bill replied detachedly, giving the incorrectly receptacled beverage his full attention. '...Actually, you know what, I'll have a pint of *Guinness*...if it's not too much trouble, darlin-g?'

'...No, that's no trouble at all, sir. At least I know where that is!' Lucy took a pint glass from the rack above her head and thumbed it clumsily. 'You were saying?'

26

'I was, wasn't I.' Bill had lit his cigarette and was following the trail of its smokescreen. '...So anyway, this firm is pretty savvy - one of the sharpest they've seen in a decade, they say. CID have been sent in.'

'CID?' Lucy asked, her eyebrows arched.

'Criminal Investigation Detectives,' the man replied with dramatic enunciation. He placed a small handful of coppers down on the bar as he spoke. 'They take root in the area for a few weeks, plant themselves in shallow soil so to speak, then knock off a few joints and off they ride into the sunset.'

The pint of *Guinness* Lucy placed in front of Bill was a misty mess.

'Right, I'm with you, officer. So you're basically on the lookout for people who are fairly new in town - is that it?'

'Oh yes, that's certainly it, young lady. Anyway, cheers! And get one for yourself.'

'I might have one later, if you don't mind. Y'know, when I'm off duty.'

'You are a good girl, aren't you?' Bill chuckled.

'Yeah, but you can give me the money now.'

She grinned at her customer, and he grinned back.

Bill lit up another *Silk Cut* as he waited for the pint to settle - you couldn't rush these things. He drank half of it unhurriedly, taking in the atmosphere of regency tiling and old timber frames...then he straightened up decisively and nodded at the barmaid.

'Time to get back on the beat. Might see you again, young lady.'

'Hope to see you again, officer,' Lucy called to the back of Bill's head as he exited. 'Be careful out there, won't you.' She poured herself an orange juice.

It didn't take a genius to work out that CID didn't walk into pubs and announce their covert strategy. Lucy the barmaid knew that, but then Lucy the barmaid was CID. And it was Criminal Investigation Department, not 'Criminal Investigation Detectives'. She suspected she wouldn't see Bill again, although she really did hope to.

'He called me "darlin",' DC Philippa Lucey told her Sergeant that evening in a back room of Ilford Constabulary. She looked smart and sharp in her police uniform. 'Officers of the law don't call a barmaid "darlin", and nor should they. Fatal error,' she said with cold derision.

As for 'Bill', he got back to the lockup on Dyke Street an hour later, stolen police tie just visible beneath his overalls, and told the rest of the lads it was time to scarper.

'They've got eyes on the Stag, I reckon,' he said, the sound of Bow Bells ringing clearly in his voice now. 'Might need to get our bees 'n honey some other place, lads. Ya shoulda seen what she done pulling that pint of *Guinness*, it was a right palaver.' He took a long drag on his cigarette.

'Only a f***ing old bill would do something that criminal if you ask me.'

five

THE BOY WHO COULD BE ANYTHING

There was once a young man whose teacher taught him that identity is there to be created; that he could be whoever or whatever he wanted.

'Write your next essay on this!' the teacher told the class.

The young man was taken with the idea that he could be whoever or whatever he wanted.

'Today I am identifying as an illiterate,' he said. 'Therefore, I shall not be able to write an essay.'

'Excellent!' said the teacher, and gave him top marks.

The next day, his parents told him that identity was there to be created; that he could be whoever or whatever he wanted.

'Now go and tidy your room!'

The young man was now even more taken with the idea that he could be whoever or whatever he wanted.

'I am currently identifying as the Venus di Milo statue,' he said. 'I have no arms, and so I shall not be able to tidy my room.'

'You do you!' His parents beamed with pride, and they tidied his room for him.

The following day on the way to school, the young man stopped by a delicatessen, which always had fine smells emanating from it. He spied a large piece of Stilton lying on a board and, hungry from not being able to eat last night because he had no arms, he gobbled up the whole lot.

'Oi!' cried the shopkeeper, 'You shall have to pay for that.'

'I shall not,' replied the boy, with confidence. 'Both my teacher and my parents have told me that I can be whoever or whatever I want to be. Today, I am identifying as a mouse, therefore I am not subjected to human laws or currency.'

The shopkeeper looked thoughtful.

'A very clever young man,' he said, walking out from behind the counter. 'As it happens, today I am identifying as a feral cat...'

And he bit down hard on the young man's neck. Within minutes, the young man had bled out.

The shopkeeper, being a mere cat, was never charged with murder.

six

AND I STILL DO

Do you know, I come back here every year, just once a year, to celebrate that moment I chose you - the moment I let the universe know that I was yours to keep.

Did you not know that?

If we walk down this bank, there's a path off to the right that takes us along the beach and then back up, past the war monument and eventually back here. I've got a picnic in the car for later.

I already was by that point, of course - yours, I mean. My heart had been straining and stretching for a while. And then when you came to that event I was singing at, and you brought your friend and he left but you stayed, you stayed and you walked down the aisle of chairs towards me and sat by me on the stage, right next to me, and you said - do you remember? - you said, 'You did alright there, lass...' When you did that, that was it for me.

Did you know that was the moment? Have you heard me tell that story? Yes, I'm sure.

Anyway, it was. And the following day I walked along this beach and I just thought, yeah, I don't want anyone else. And I said to the sky, to God, to whoever - 'If redemption looks like him then I believe in redemption.' And I still do.

Our messages increased after that, didn't they? And I was like Pavlov's Dog every time my phone pinged - is it him, has he texted? And obviously it was you. It was always you. Staying up late every night chatting and giggling, seeing how long I could keep you there before you needed to sleep. It was so nice just to have someone to talk to and laugh with before bed. And then I'd read back through all of our messages from that evening and just relive the conversation again.

I remember this bench, we've had a picnic here. I can't remember when...

Then you sent that voice note while you were driving, to tell me about something you heard on the radio and you said I should listen to it. It was about the psychology of love. 'Love', you said, and I can still hear you saying it in your lovely voice. You still have the same lovely voice today, I think. No, you really do.

I began dropping you into conversations after that. 'I was saying to a friend of mine,' I'd say, or 'let me tell you something I heard about love'. I started showing pictures of you, too. My brother told me you looked identical to Vince, and my sister-in-law agreed. I stopped showing pictures of you after that.

Here's the bandstand. It looks like it's been repainted since last time, doesn't it?

Do you remember the first selfie you sent me? No? You were wearing that garishly purple cycling jacket that you loved so much. I could draw that photo from memory - the raised eyebrows, the cheeky smile. You still have the same smile, you do - stop it, you're not old!

And it was here that you first kissed me. By this bandstand, or maybe down there on the beach. But you kissed me and I kissed you, and we said 'I love you'. Maybe we got our shoes wet and we couldn't stop laughing.

Of course, by that point you had told me that we couldn't message any more; that she had hacked your phone and she wanted to kill me. You weren't even together by that point but she was using anything to punish you, to stop you seeing your boys. And I needed to keep you safe.

So I met my friend Julie in the pub and I just wept. I wept and I wept, because I knew that was it: that the sun had stopped in the sky; that she would always be around and would always hate me and hate you if I was around. So I had to continue our story without you after that. But it was still our story. It always has been *our* story.

Those houses are new, I think, aren't they? Change is inevitable, I suppose.

So you blocked me…and I kissed you anyway. And I told you that I loved you anyway, because I wanted to say it and I wanted you to hear it. And you said 'I love you too', and you said 'love' just like in that message about psychology. You have always said it like that, every day since then for twenty years. I love hearing you say 'love'.

Here's the war monument, still nicely preserved. 'They shall not grow old as we who are left grow old. Time shall not weary them…'

So many happy times. That night in Majorca, under the stars.

Mark told me that you'd moved away. So did I, eventually.

Driving through Scotland and laughing at me because I couldn't do the accent, that weekend in the log cabin.

I saw a picture a year later where you had put your wedding ring back on. Why did you do that?

And just those lovely cosy evenings alone, together, having the same conversations we had in the beginning, over and over, always the same conversations. Just perfect.

I heard that you did eventually remarry. I never did. I have been ever faithful to you. I did date some people, but I couldn't give them my heart because it doesn't belong to them.

There was so much I wanted to say to you.

And I have done, every day for two decades.

What a pair, hey? Perfect for each other, aren't we? This is where the loop finishes - the car's just over there, we've gone in a circle.

I just wanted to say thank you. And to tell you that you're as handsome and ideal as you were back then, when you sat on that stage next to me and you said, 'You did alright there, lass.' Don't go changing, my darling, are you listening?

The last twenty years have been amazing, love. I just hope that, wherever you are and whatever you've been up to, you've enjoyed them too.

seven

WINE IN WHISKEY GLASSES

When I looked up I hadn't expected to see a woman standing in the window. She was looking down at me curiously, but she didn't wave or smile and perhaps she didn't see me. But then she left the window where she had been framed and made a slow descent to find me. It was her house and she was allowed to be there after all.

She came out into the garden where I was sitting with a pencil and a pad - which had sentences that couldn't quite couple with other sentences, which was annoying - and she sat down quite close to me and brought an over-full carafe of wine in to land on the table, with two whiskey glasses inscribed with 'To the happy couple' and a date on them.

'Wine in whiskey glasses?' I asked, and she said she didn't know the difference and shrugged as though she didn't care, though I think she might have. And I stopped writing and we started talking together as the early evening of the early summer, which makes everything pleasant and makes everyone feel safe, enshrined us. She was maybe twenty years older than me, recently widowed, and it showed in her face and in the way she walked. I was recently divorced - had been forever, it felt like - and perhaps that showed in my face too, although I didn't talk about it unless someone asked, and even then not very far or very deep.

'The garden is always growing,' she said. 'I can't keep up with it.'

It was more like a meadow than a garden, and it was wild and quite wondrous as most of the New Forest is - a good place to come and write stories about new things and old things; things that grew wild or got tended to so that they didn't.

'Would you like a cigarette?' she asked and I said I didn't smoke, which hadn't always been true and I think she caught that somewhere in my expression.

'You may if you like,' she said, pouring us both another glass of whiskey-wine, which was cheap and past its best but it was there and it was free. And so I did have a cigarette, but only one, and then another one after that, watching the smoke drift wherever it wanted and then disappear into somewhere or nowhere.

And we talked for a long time in the depths of that old new forest, her telling me about how the garden used to be, complaining about the Japanese Knotweed and saying 'It kills gardens as you know', when I didn't know that at all. And I told her about the story I was writing, and how I couldn't find the right ending and I was using too many adverbs which were killing it.

'Like Japanese Knotweed,' she said, and I laughed at that.

In the morning before I left I would help her move a table, and I would tell her how I had started writing another story and had already finished it and it had Japanese Knotweed in it, and she would say, 'Thank you'. But for now we sat in the meadow-garden and drank our wine and smoked our cigarettes, and talked like people who haven't lost their husbands and still have their wives. And she told me what starlings sound like, though I've since forgotten, and I told her about my books and she listened even though she hadn't asked.

But then it was dark and the light had decayed and she said, 'I'm going up to bed now. Don't stay up too late.' And I said I wouldn't but I might sit here a little longer and let the edge of night sharpen my pencil. So she took a match and lit the small table lantern for me. And then she was back inside and the blackness was here and cold and the lantern was powerless. And the woman at the window looked out towards me from the fond light of her bedroom, but she wouldn't have seen me. And then she closed her curtains and it was as though she wasn't there either.

Part 2:
NIGHT

eight

FOOTPRINTS

One day, a man had a dream. He was walking along a sandy beach, thinking back over his life. Seagulls laughed as they hovered overhead and the warm light of the sun broke into a million kaleidoscopic shards against the incoming tide. Presently, another figure drew level with him and began to walk alongside.

'Welcome, Lord,' said the man whose dream it was. 'I am seeing you for the first time, but I know that you have been walking close to me all of my life.'

'You are quite correct,' replied the figure, 'although perhaps you are also mistaken.'

The two men walked together along the flat shore, the tide slowly creeping up towards its breakline. As they did so, scenes from the man's life began to flash across the sky in perfect detail. He watched them unfold as he walked, sometimes feeling his heart inflate in his chest at points of romantic intimacy, at other points feeling a drag in his stomach during times of shame and tragedy. As the final scene faded, the man looked back along the featureless beach and noticed that only one set of footprints was visible. His face creased with consternation as he turned to his travelling companion.

'Lord, how can it be that as I look back over my life I see only one set of footprints?'

'Look again,' the figure said. The man whose dream it was looked back, but once again he saw only one set of footprints - and something even more disturbing.

'Lord, why is it that I see only one set of footprints? And why are they yours?'

The figure's eyes flashed with humour.

'Do you not understand? The reason you see only one set of footprints is because your life has left no imprint whatsoever.'

The dreaming man stopped walking and turned towards his companion. This was not the conversation he had expected.

'Pardon?' he said. 'What do you mean?'

'I simply mean that the sands of time have been left completely undisturbed by your existence.' The figure's tone was as flat as the shoreline.

'But I don't understand. Shouldn't you be saying that it was because you were carrying me through hard times?'

'You mistake me,' said the Lord. 'I have never carried you. I have merely stalked you, and finally, now at the end, I have caught up to you.'

'The end? But Lord, this is not fair. Please, show mercy.'

'I have told you already: you mistake me.' The words sounded like they were coming through a tangle of rotted seaweed. 'And Lord Death is deaf to appeal.'

At this, Lord Death placed a gentle, cold hand on the man's face. He felt a sweet tingling as every atom in his body fizzed and bubbled into a billion grains of sand. For a split second, the man looked like a beautifully crafted sand castle. Then he disintegrated into sorrowful blackness.

Lord Death looked back at where his deep, implacable footprints had made their unhurried march up the beach. He smiled at the sound of the seagulls laughing and the warmth of the sun on his skinless skull. Then he looked down the beach to where an elderly lady was walking her dog, and smiled. He marched on, his booted foot crunching hard into the small mound of sand that used to be a person.

The man woke up from his dream with a start. A beach ball had landed on him from where some children were playing football nearby. He sat up, breathing heavily and with bulbous beads of sweat flowing down his face. Waking reality reasserted itself - he was on holiday. He was just on holiday.

'Are you OK?' his wife asked.

'Yeah, yeah - I just had a weird dream.'

'Too much Sangria, probably.'

'Yeah, that's probably it. Or might have a bit of sunstroke. I'm just going for a paddle to snap myself out of it.'

'Have fun,' his wife said, returning to her book by Ray Bradbury.

He dusted sand off his towel as he stood and took a drink of water. Seagulls laughed overhead. The man who had been asleep walked down to where the hard, moist sand framed the receding tide, then he wandered along the sealine towards the pier. As he did so, he thought back over his life just as he had done in his dream, various scenes flashing through his mind as though on a big screen. A dog sprinted past him into the waves, its elderly owner struggling to keep up, the animal's leash jangling at his side.

'Excuse me, can you stop him please?' the owner called weakly.

The man splashed into the small waves and carefully scooped up the dog, whose silver nametag rapped against his knuckles.

'Good boy, good boy, calm down. Let your master catch up.' He read the dog's name tag. 'Just wait here, Grimmy.'

Presently, the dog's owner drew alongside and reached out both arms in triumph.

'You didn't think you could escape that easily, did you, boy?'

The man holding the dog chuckled. 'How far could he have got?'

'Oh, not far,' replied Lord Death, the leash swaying below his fleshless hand. 'Not very far at all.'

nine

STRAWBERRY PICKING

really think I might marry this one. She is decidedly prettier than she realises, and maybe her self-confessed 'acursedness' in matters of the heart has caused her to lower her sights to someone like myself. That is fine by me, and I am ready to shake firmly by the hand any of the long line of men who have supposedly been 'scared off' by some vague-but-inherently-disqualifying aspect to her personality.

'Happens all the time,' she tells me with a squinting and guarded smile over a calzone.

I gaze at her studiously, scanning her charmingly asymmetrical face for rumours of ugliness, like Egon Spengler using an aurascope to sniff out ghosts - and find nothing but rosy-cheeked splendour.

'People are just selfish and self-centred, Katie. It's only in fiction that people act rationally. I think for you to draw a line of worst fit through the immature actions of cognitively and emotionally stunted human males probably isn't good for your mental health.'

I fix her with mock severity, then let a boyish chuckle pop the pompousness of what I've said. She smiles.

'You're very good with words,' she says, almost reverently. 'I suppose you know that, what with you being a writer.'

'Yes. I am and I do. I'm very careful with my words and you're the prettiest girl I know.' She smiles again as a single onion layer of insecurity peels away. Maybe that's what she likes about me - my artistry with words, my commitment to telling the truth through story. Maybe she's reassured that I wouldn't silently and wordlessly ghost her, without explanation, without a final chapter. She says that has happened so many times and I believe she's right about me. I love stories too much to leave any tale without a final chapter.

So I agree to meet her family, at a Christening for one of her nephews, and afterwards at the garden party her mother is hosting. Katie's family is vast and tendrily, and she claims, maybe only half-joking, that she doesn't know most of them, but it means I won't be overly scrutinised or quizzed and we can disapparate if necessary.

'Mum had seven kids - I mean, who does that? We used to say that she started with me and kept going until she got it right!'

I tell her I'm an only child and so my parents obviously didn't think I could be improved upon.

'Just be aware that they have a tendency to overshare. It's what happens when you have such a large family and it becomes a mini-society all by itself.'

I assure her that I will stay alert.

It's a molten hot day as we crunch to a gentle halt on the post-Christening gravel drive. The old family farm house is sprawling and unstately, not unlike the family. Not run-down so much as

46

frayed around the edges: brittle outer brick walls bulging with history; rooms stuffed with forgotten tales. I tell Katie I'm a bit nervous to enter her ancestral home, although it isn't true. I'm always looking for a new story, a new character; always looking for a way in.

The lobby is whitewashed and chilly, with photos and canvases, large and diminutive, identity-parading the family along the hallway to where the kitchen gapes like a wide mouth. The red-brick reminds me of a pizza oven in this heat as I follow Katie out into the orchard behind the annex, splitting my time between admiring her bum and selecting a suitable swagger from my wardrobe of first impressions. Katie's mother is sitting in a camping chair cradling a bundle of cloud-white cotton that must contain the baby. She welcomes me and bids me agree with her that the Christening was lovely, and I do agree. I say it was joyous in its muted reverence, using my clever words and drawing a smirk of faux chastisement from Katie.

'You must be the famous storyteller,' one of her sisters says, and I recognise her as Joanne, the Mother of the baptised who I noticed at the Christening.

'Oh, you'll find some stories here, young man!' Katie's mother exclaims, scanning her assorted offspring with nefarious satisfaction. 'Don't say too much, everyone, or he'll put you in his next book!' Self-indulgent laughter breaks out like blossom.

Of the gathered folk, I half-recognise a few from social media. A chap juggling a single apple is, I think, Katie's youngest brother. A couple sitting on a picnic rug are another brother and his wife, freshly dipped with holiday tannage. A much paler girl standing under the eaves of a tree looks like a blonder version of Katie and must be another sister. She gives me a cartoonish wave when I look over at her. I look back a minute later and she repeats the act, supplementing the gawky wave with a gleeful, garish smile.

Canapés are passed around and cider is sluiced from oak kegs. I sit under a leafy canopy and absorb - or am absorbed by - the familial banter, lore and legend. And Katie sits beside me, breaking down a Victoria sponge with her fork - a cake which looks more sturdy than the bricks holding the house together. Two ciders in and she drapes her warm hair over my bald head, and I see her mother drape a smile over the two of us; a smile that says 'Aw…finally.' And in my mind I am setting scenes, conjuring words and carving sentences, future-casting our first child's Christening, giving body to the ghost of an idea, which is how all writing starts.

Three ciders in and I excuse myself, melting away from the mad in-crowd and slipping back into the kitchen where the air is cold and the chill of red brick soothes like a flannel. The blonde girl is already in there and, inhibitions lowered from homebrewed apples, I offer the same theatrical wave that she gave me in the orchard.

'So nice to meet you,' she says with incredible enthusiasm.

'Are you…one of the sisters?' I ask, my voice inflecting to an uncharitable height.

'I'm her sister, Rebecca. And you are Phil, and you tell stories for a living. Soooo nice.' She is chuckling and I don't know why.

'Did we meet at the Christening?' I ask, and she shakes her head.

'Not my thing, Phil, the famous storyteller.'

I tell her that I'm not famous at all and I don't just write stories, but articles and other bits and bobs.

'Bits and bobs,' she repeats, her eyes full of a confusing mischief. 'But you like the stories the best, I bet, don't you? You like telling stories.'

I try to drum up candour in my response, but I feel like something is coming - something unseen.

'They allow for the most creativity, for sure. And you don't have to tell the truth, of course.'

'Oh, but you must!' Rebecca declares through a broken smile, cracked like mortar. 'If you don't tell the truth, how will we enjoy the story?'

I start to embark on a clarification to my words: that I think all fiction must be at least emotionally true, even if the literal facts are reworked…but Rebecca speaks over me, her mirth returning too abruptly to seem genuine, as though she had plucked it from the utensil rack above the *Aga*.

'You must get Katie to tell you a story, Phil.'

'Oh really?' The girl is staring at me with a singular fascination - the fascination of someone peeling plaster off a wall.

'What sort of story should I ask her to tell?'

'Yes, you must get her to tell you a story - a good one! One about strawberry picking. Ask her about that. Ask her about the time she went strawberry picking, Phil. And make sure she tells the truth.' Rebecca has dissolved into such girlish and incongruous giggles that I decide to leave her to whatever fermented fruit she's been abusing.

'Oh Ok, I'll tell you then,' she says as I turn to leave. '...One summer Katie went strawberry picking. Didn't she.' Her humour falls off a cliff.

'Uh, I don't know, I don't...'

'She did, Phil, she did go strawberry picking and if you want to be a famous storyteller then you need to know the story. She did go strawberry picking, Phil, but do you know...she picked something else as well. Something that was mine. And I have never forgiven her for that.'

Like an apple hurled against masonry, Rebecca explodes with a sudden, horrible glee. 'I suspect I never will, Phil.'

I stand confused, rubbing my thumb back and forth along a worktop. 'Is that...is that the story?'

'Oh, you must get her to tell you the story! It'll be such a laugh, go on, promise me that you'll force her to tell you the story.'

I tell Rebecca that I'm desperate for the toilet. The descending trill of 'tell you a story...' follows me down the hallway like toilet paper on the bottom of one's shoe.

Hometime is a relief, and not simply because of the aircon.

'You met my family, then. Still interested?'

I laugh at the genuine question lodged like loose mortar between two blocks of irony. I give Katie a reassuring rub on the arm as I navigate the grey vein of the b-road. 'You do have quite a family.'

'I tried to tell you! You could write a whole novel on them, I bet!'

'Indeed, yes! Yes I could…and I could put in a chapter about strawberry picking if you like.'

Katie has been watching the country lanes recede but now half-turns back towards me.

'Who told you that?' she asks, amusement and irascibility battling it out for dominance of her features.

'Let's just say it was one of your sisters?' I say, my intonation once again so broken that it turns a statement into a question.

'And I bet I know which one as well! I told you my family was prone to oversharing, didn't I?!'

'You did, yes, but don't worry - I haven't heard any details.'

'Good,' she replies, and I sit patiently for ten seconds.

'…Can I hear the story though?'

'No!'

'Oh please, Katie, please. "And make sure she tells the truth," your sister said.'

'There is no story! I don't know why she would bring it up. Every single boyfriend I've had for the last ten years has been forced into asking me about it, and it's not even a good story!'

I tell Katie it's a twenty-minute drive and I'm not putting any music on until she tells the story. She huffs and puffs and eventually concedes.

'All it is, is this. When I finished uni I came back here for the summer while I worked out what I wanted to do. There were some jobs going picking strawberries, so I thought I'll get a bit of money and work on my tan - bonus! There was a guy there called Dean who was dating Rebecca - I don't know if I've told you about her but she was my sister who died - and anyway, Dean and I kissed and had a bit of a fling, and so I told Joanne and she said, "Find another job and don't tell Rebecca!" So that's it really. What can I say, I used to play the field a bit.'

I have taken my foot off the accelerator and pull off the road in response to a sign that says 'Escape Lane 100 yards'. I put on the handbrake and stare ahead of me into a thick copse of pine, dark in summer shade.

Katie asks what the matter is and I ask her if she did eventually tell Rebecca the truth. She says that she never did and that her sister died in a coach crash less than a year later.

'Is that the story you were wanting to hear?' she asks.

'...No, that wasn't...'

'...I told you, it's not a story - there's no ending to it. Look, are you OK?'

I tell her I'm fine and merge back onto the carriageway. I put some music on for the rest of the journey.

I drop Katie back at her house and she gives me a big wave and says she'll see me next time.

But she won't. She will never hear from me again.

ten

KUEBIKO

(Longlisted for the Creative Writing Ink prize)

Here you come, with that slightly loping gait of yours - arms swinging and joy bringing - the world receding under your feet. I watch you as you come, never turning my head. I see only you. The heat of the sun seeps through the woven fibres of my hat and makes me feel alive, and so I am, because you are coming for me. The ground between us is baked and cracked but my heart is whole and full - filled by you.

You have something for me - a gift. You have given me so many gifts: a scarf, a waistcoat, life itself, a nose. You are my provider and I, my love, I am your protector. With me you are safe. Not like with him.

By day I keep the beasts of the skies from your fields, so that you may eat well and put down deep roots. I fling my enemies hence with outstretched arms sleeved in tweed. I conjure sunlight and blind my foes with reflected glory that bounces and flashes from cufflink and buckle and button.

But when the sun turns it's back, my love, then, then I keep you safe from The Other: from the pestilence that stalks by night and from the evil that creeps and encroaches. For I also have deep roots; roots that go back and further back and still back - further than you can remember - to my father, Priapus.

My kin has been here almost as long as yours, and I know the deep stories. I feel them, here below the ground where you thrust me and birthed me. The rocks cry out and the soil whispers to me and I could tell you stories, my love, oh yes I could - if you would only give me a voice. You made me smile the other day: the corners of my mouth upturned by your kindness and by your pen. But can you give me a voice before it is too late? Will you? I long to cry for you; to draw you like a mother to her child; to lull and lure you like the Bubak. To tell you a story, before the real darkness comes.

Here you are, then. You greet me, your lips vivid and vital.

'Hey, hay-man, my He-Man,' you say, and you stroke my face, soft flesh on warm hessian. You look into my eyes and I do not look away. I will never look away from you.

'You're so handsome, Mr Feathertop,' you tell me, though I do not know if you are telling the truth or just telling me a story. You call me 'Mr Feathertop,' and maybe that's from a story too, but not one that I know. Perhaps that's a story that lives in a book, but I only know the stories that live in the earth - stories much deeper than any of your books. Stories that fossilise but never die.

'You're the only man I trust, hay-man,' you say. 'If they only had a brain, right?'

And then you, who filled my very heart, pour out yours before me. You tell me how He mistreats you; how He grabs you and scares you and makes you want to fly from Him. Your sorrow spills into the earth and joins our two stories together, just for a moment. I wish to fling Him hence; to terrify Him like the bloodless carrion that He is. I wish to fold you into my arms and absorb all of your grief; for your tears to seep into my grain and your shame to hang on my frame. For there is power in two pieces of wood nailed, my love, or do you not know that story? Is it not written in one of your books?

'You're so easy to talk to, Mr Feathertop,' you tell me through your cultivating tears. 'I can be myself with you. Nothing scares the scarecrow.'

Oh, but you are wrong, my love. You are very wrong. Give me my voice and I will tell you how wrong you are. Open my mouth, my love, and you will hear my story. *Give me my voice.*

'See you tomorrow, hay-man. Keep smiling,' you say, and then you turn away. I watch you retreat, the world and my world retreating with you. You are going back to Him: He who swoops in and picks the meat from your spirit; He who harvests your heart and spits the kernels out; whose encircling shadow signals decay.

You will return to me tomorrow as you always do. I will feel your coming as tremors in the ground and I will watch your approach with false smile and glassy eyes. And I will stand my ground for you. But I know that we cannot be together. You can never truly commit to me, even after all you have done and all we have been. And before winter comes, my love, you will do one final thing for me: you will burn me. You will burn me with your love, and the flames of desire and longing will light up the night sky and my enemies will quake and quail before my furious flaming love. And you will scatter my hopes over mud and manure and the earth will have another secret - another untold story. And you will have burned the one who loved you, as you save and preserve The Other. But this is not the refining fire of that old, old story. And when the Spring comes, then you will take another lover, for it could not have been any other way. Remember that I know the deep stories. And you will dress him in my clothes and paint him with smiles and you will not remember me. And you will never hear my voice, for I will not be here to use it. And who then will be left to save you from Him?

And that, my love, if I were able to speak through this hessian mouth…that, I would tell you, is what truly scares the scarecrow.

eleven

THE PERPLEXITY OF THE HOUSE ON MALLEUS ROAD

"Ok, so we'd been in the house on Malleus Road for about three weeks, I suppose. Term had restarted but only just...so yeah, about three weeks. And I hadn't seen Bella for about twenty-four hours, which was odd because she never worked that hard so the idea of her tied to her desk studying wasn't, you know...didn't seem likely.

I went and knocked on her door and found her sitting upright but like in the foetal position, you know, just on her bed, with a coat over her knees, sort of like at those outdoor concerts that my parents go to. I asked her what the matter was and she told me she was 'cold and depressed', those were her words. She didn't know why, couldn't work it out, and I thought it was odd, you know, because we weren't freshers any more, you know - the workload and being away from home wasn't a novelty...and because, well, she didn't seem prone to bouts of depression or mental health issues - not that there's anything wrong with that, it just wasn't...it didn't really fit her personality.

Anyway, she was like this for a couple of days and I just had this sense that it might have something to do with lack of natural light or something. That room was on the ground floor at the back of the house, and the yard had quite a high wall that meant it was always fairly dark. So I just offered to swap because, you know, I went home most weekends and, like, was often at my boyfriend's house to sleep over, whereas Bella was there the whole time, in Manchester, so I just thought it made sense.

And honestly, Bella's mood changed almost overnight - dramatically - and she was back to being normal Bella, you know, belting out Madonna and leaving a huge mess everywhere. And I didn't suffer any change or lowering of my mood. I made sure to take Vitamin D supplements just in case, but I was fine...it was fine. For about a week.

Then, one evening - I reckon now it must have been between 9pm and 10pm, although I only know that with hindsight of course - I was writing an essay, when all of a sudden I hear this bloody great scream in the corridor outside my room. I nearly s*** myself first of all, and then I race into the hall...but there's nobody there. And I'm like, whaaaat? Cos Bella was in her room - my old room - at the top of the house, but she had her headphones in. And our other flatmate, Molly (Molly Whitehouse) hadn't moved in at that point so it was just the two of us, me and Bel. So I'm proper freaked out by this, you know, as you can imagine, but I sort of decided it had to be the lads next door - it's another student house and a load of boys, so...but it really sounded like it was from outside my door, so I'm pretty confused. But then the more I thought about it, I kind of convinced myself it was a trick of the acoustics.

Nothing happens for another week. And then the following Monday, again between 9 and 10, I hear the sound of scuffling in the hall - same place as the scream. And it sounds like too many people just in a narrow corridor, trying to push past each other. Really weird. But then I hear the sound of like fists scraping and thudding on the walls which, you know…really f****** creepy. I thought it must be Bella and her mates back - she'd been off out at one of the society socials, or so she told me - so I opened the door ready to shout 'Keep that noise down!' like some sort of angry parent, you know, shouting up the stairs in a movie. Only the corridor was empty. There was nobody there.

But that wasn't the worst bit. The scariest thing was that the scuffling and, you know, the banging - the fists and all that - it didn't stop. It went down the corridor. But not fast, not panicked. It took its time. And I could see where it was…no, I couldn't see it, but I could *sense* it. And I could tell where it was because of where the walls were banging and the carpet…the carpet was moving. And then at the end of the corridor it stopped - and then the kitchen door opened.

And I just, man, I just legged it. I was out of there like a flash.

I didn't go back to that house for a week. I wouldn't go in, wouldn't go near it. I rang Bella and she must have thought - well, she did think - that I'd just properly lost it. And, you know, I smoked a bit of weed that term, but not that much! And anyway, not on that day - I only had it when my boyfriend came round 'cos it was his…you know, he arranged it. So anyway, Bella spoke to the landlord about it, and I don't think he said very much other than offering to change the locks if we wanted. But I didn't need to keep stuff out. It was what was already inside the house that was the problem, you know. It was the house - it was something in the house.

Right, Part 3 then…and to be honest, OK, if I would have known the real goings-on at the time, I would never have stuck around for what finally happened, you know. No way - I would have been long gone in Acapulco or somewhere. But events just unfolded in this weird way.

I was taking a little nap before pulling an all-nighter, OK, so again it's between 9pm and 10pm, when I heard a loud smash from the kitchen, followed by the sound of frantic footsteps going up the stairs.

So I shout up, 'Are you OK, Bel?' No response.

I go into the kitchen and find my nice cafetière lying on the floor in about a million pieces. First thought, obviously, is 'How am I going to get the necessary caffeine to get my through this essay?' But I'll worry about that later, I thought. But I'm confused because Bella didn't drink coffee, and it had obviously been thrown, the way it had spread across the floor, the shards of glass - it wasn't an accident. So I'm feeling really angry and pissed off, but I thought 'Stay calm' and I went up to see what was going on. Bella opens her door in a flood of tears, shuddering and, you know, body spasming.

I say, 'What's happened?' you know, 'What's the matter?'

And she sits me down on her bed and tells me this long story about how she's been sleeping with a guy who was engaged, and how news has got out and this guy's fiancée's brother was threatening to kill the bloke and to come and find Bella. And you know, you know what students are like - it all sounds like guff and bravado to me, people threatening to kill each other, whatever, Manchester University mafia bulls***. So I joke that maybe we do need those new locks from the landlord after all, at which I got a laugh.

OK, so we chatted for a while until she's stopped shuddering, and then I said, 'Don't worry about the cafetiere, it's just a cheap one,' at which she says 'OK' but looks a little bit confused, you see? Well, I know now, don't I, why that was - she'd been in her room the whole time, and the frantic footsteps up the stairs weren't hers.

The fact she was in such a state and really upset was just a coincidence…or maybe not, I don't know. I don't know what I think about that bit still.

OK, deep breaths. Sorry if I'm rambling, I'm just trying to get it all in the right order. Are you ready? OK, Part 4 - final part.

Two days later, Thursday night, somewhere between 9pm and 10pm, I come back down the corridor from the kitchen with a pack of biscuits after washing up and putting everything away. OK, to be really clear - I put *everything* away. I'm like Mrs. Hinch when I get started, me.

As soon as I open my bedroom door I just see this guy climbing in through the open window. No idea how he got in, it was late November in Manchester - there are zero open windows! But seriously, you've seen the window, I've shown you - Upvc sliding sash. The key was in my sock drawer and I am sure I had locked it, but I can't have done, and there's a good chance I just thought I'd locked it and maybe unlocked it by mistake, you know - I'm not great with DIY and stuff.

So I see this guy and I just kind of fall back into the corridor with a scream. OK? A *scream*. Remember the first thing I told you about was the scream in the corridor? Well, this guy looks startled, as you do, but he's in now and maybe he just thinks 'I'm committed now'. So he just says…sort of growls, 'Are you Bella?' and I say, 'No, I'm not,' but he clearly doesn't believe me and so he chases me into the corridor and grabs hold of me. At this point I'm so scared - it's a tiny narrow place as you've seen so there's no way he can really swing for me and the most he can do is start pushing me against the wall, but it was…honestly, it was horrific. But then from nowhere, from like out of the walls it seemed, I just felt this sense of fierceness come over me. It was as though this external force had filled the corridor and was pressing down on me, but not to suffocate me - to give me strength, if that makes sense. So I just start trying to hit this guy, and he's trying to pin me to the wall but I don't feel scared any more - and I totally promise you, I'm a major coward, OK? I'm a lover not a fighter, so to say.

So he's grappling me and I'm jabbing him and we're causing all these bangs, OK, and the only thing I can really do is retreat down the corridor with him manhandling me and calling me this, that and the other, stuff I won't repeat, but every name under the sun basically. Bella's upstairs with her music on but I can't call her can I, cos he's here for her, isn't he. But I just feel so calm and almost zen at this point, I don't think to cry out for help, you know - even though I'm not, you know, I'm not winning the wrestling match or whatever it is.

Anyway, we get into the kitchen and somehow I pull myself free. And then this bloke looks at me, insane with rage, and he starts calling me a bitch and how I've ruined his little sister's life. I tell him I haven't and he calls me a liar and he looks now like he is going to properly fly at me. And then I see the cafetière, the one I just put away. And I remember the smash from the previous night, and then I remember the scuffling and banging that moved down the corridor that made me flee, and the scream on that first evening…and I realise…I realise it's everything that's happened - or, if it hasn't happened yet, what is *going* to happen. And so I just - quite calmly - I just pick up this cafetiere by the handle, and as he comes for me I swing it, it hits him in the head, smashes, he goes down clutching his face, glass goes everywhere…and then I do just bolt it out of the kitchen and up the stairs, into Bella's room without an explanation, lock the door and call the police."

That was the (slightly edited) transcript from the interview recording I took of Aggie McBride just over two years ago. In over fifteen years of researching the paranormal and supernatural, it is - or was - one of the most fascinating cases I've looked into.

Aggie emailed me the day after I went to meet her at the house on Malleus Road, and reaffirmed what she had said about the events concerned. Moreover, she was adamant in her conclusion that the house itself, or potentially some presence within the house, had acted with conscious benevolence to protect and help her and her roommate, Bella. Whilst I only managed a brief chat with Bella, and whilst she was unable to comment on what she didn't witness, she was however able to corroborate both the attack and the preternatural sense of calm displayed by Aggie. She also vouched for Aggie's mental stability and general trustworthiness.

Several things made this case so singular. Firstly, the predictive, foretelling nature of the events leading up to the attack. In none of the hundreds of cases with which I've dealt first-hand has there ever been a positively prophetic aspect to a haunting. It is not uncommon for victims of paranormal activity to witness premonitions (dreams which harbinge doom, for example), but such premonitions have a supremely low success rate as score predictors; that is, they almost never come true. Coupled with that is the contention that the spirit or energy within the house was somehow helping, somehow constructive (Aggie described it as 'Home Alone on steroids'). The early stages of the events described in Aggie's account tally perfectly with what one might call a standard poltergeist encounter. But the foreknowledge of what was to follow and the sympathetic benevolence of the spirit (the provision of the cafetiere which Aggie was certain had previously been cleared away; the emotional manipulation that saw Bella move out of the room that was eventually infiltrated) if true, push the case away from the paranormal and into the realm of the angelic. One might ask why a knife wasn't provided instead an unwieldy glass receptacle, but this only adds weight to the idea of a benevolent spirit, who would want to use reasonable, but not fatal, force.

That angelic storyline was certainly the conclusion Aggie had reached, and it was one I was fond of as a nice counterbalance to the standard haunting experience. Even after interviewing a Vicar specialising in so-called deliverance ministry (Rev. John ***** of the Manchester Diocese), who repudiated the idea of an angelic being supporting violence or causing depression, and who stated that angels are personal beings rather than simply non-verbal presences leaving clues, the 'friendly ghost' hypothesis still struck me as viable within the context.

What causes me to revise that theory, and the reason for writing this blog now, is the revelation of events that have occurred in that house, 60 Malleus Road, in the two years since Aggie's time there.

Three weeks ago, I got a ping on *******, a piece of software that trawls online news sites and alerts you to references of flagged phrases. I had Malleus Road flagged but initially didn't react - the nature of the news article is irrelevant to the software, so a burst water main or a new pothole is the most common reason for a ping. The initial ping was from the *Manchester Evening News*, but when the phrase pinged again in the Stoke *Sentinel*, I dived in - and to my horror.

It appears that within the last month a young female student studying at Manchester University was brutally attacked and hospitalised by a male intruder. The attack happened around 9:25pm. I wasn't able to contact anyone directly involved, so I attempted to contact the landlord. I left a message on his phone and a couple of hours later I received a call from his son, who said that his father was no longer working as a private landlord and had placed that particular property on the market. The son didn't want to say very much more, but after a bit more pressing I did get some final information from him. Apparently, the recent attack was not the second time the house had been infiltrated - but the third. On each occasion the attack had happened between 9pm and 10pm. On each occasion a young lady had been attacked by a male aggressor. On each occasion the attacker had got in through the downstairs window at the back of the house. And on each occasion, the room's inhabitant was certain the window had been locked.

The most chilling piece of information the landlord's son left until last:

'Mate, after the second time it happened Dad had bars put on the downstairs windows. How the **** does someone squeeze through bars?'

'Had the bars been removed to aid entry?' I asked, trying to keep my voice steady.

'No, mate,' he replied. 'No, they hadn't.'

twelve

ON A DREAM

'Sir, can I ask you a question?'

The tall boy in the odd clothing had reached the classroom in record time. Mr Cash was sitting on a desk, sitting on his hands like a cool pupil, and seemed to have been expecting him.

'Why aren't you in school uniform, Iestyn?'

'I don't know where it is, sir,' the tall boy replied.

Mr Cash chuckled. 'What do you want to know?'

'I know you're an English teacher, sir, but you've always been my favourite so I've come to ask you. I never liked the science teachers. The only science I enjoyed was burning magnesium strips with a Bunsen burner.'

'Well, that's very kind of you!' Mr Cash replied.

'I've been musing on it recently: if someone falls asleep while driving on the motorway and then they crash, does the crash wake them up, or is it like dying in your sleep?'

Mr Cash's eyes widened at the unusual question. 'Because obviously I would know about that,' he laughed.

The summer sun was shining nostalgically in through the latticed windows. It had been dark and overcast earlier, but it was a lovely day here. Later, if he had chance, Iestyn would walk up to the golf course with Scott and Thingy and search the brambles for discarded golf balls.

Mr Cash stood up from his desk chair and starting writing on the blackboard. The squeaking and scritching of chalk was a sound one never forgets.

'It's all digital white boards now, isn't it? But you can't beat the old blackboards.'

'What are you writing, sir?'

'I'm just getting ready for Sports Day. Have you finished your essay on Keats?'

'Well, I wanted to ask for your help on that actually. I can't remember the poem.'

Mr Cash laughed again. 'It's on the whiteboard!'

Iestyn looked up and saw that, yes, there it was, scrawled in black.

'Of course! Thanks, sir, now I remember! I love that poem.'

'Hand it in tomorrow, please, or I'll have to tell Carla.'

Now it was Iestyn's turn to laugh. 'How did you know I had a girlfriend, sir? You've never taught her.'

'She told me at lunchtime in the canteen.'

Iestyn hadn't been to the canteen in years, not since he took a chance on a leek and broccoli bake which tasted like a batting glove. He was confused that Carla would have told a member of staff they were dating, but actually that was quite sweet and so the worry dissipated like an idea in a dream.

'Do you love her, do you think?' Mr Cash asked, looking from the window down into the quad, where a mass of primary school children were playing noiselessly.

'Erm…no, I don't think so. I miss Meg. Am I in trouble?'

'Meg was much prettier,' Mr Cash nodded sadly.

'I'll break up with Carla in the morning,' Iestyn vowed enthusiastically.

'Stop swerving about!' his teacher chided him.

'I'll do my essay on T.S. Eliot first!'

'Haha, star pupil!' Mr Cash said, abruptly changing his tone and giving Iestyn a standing ovation.

The door opened and in came Mrs Woodcock, Iestyn's former Cub Scout leader. She was eating a bag of Cola Bottles from the ice-cream van on the top road. The cellophane bags had a removable seal, but most kids just ripped a hole in the side and secreted the bags in their blazer pockets where the sugar and sherbert collected in the seams.

'Ooh, Mrs Woodcock, can I have a cola bottle?' Iestyn asked.

'Have a handful,' Mrs Woodcock grinned, handing him the pack. He took one and placed it into his mouth. It barely tasted of anything but that wasn't the point. 50p per bag or three bags for £1.

'Your question, then,' Mr Cash said. 'About dying in a motorway crash?'

'Yes, that's what I came in here for.'

Mrs Woodcock looked fantastic. He'd always thought of her as being pretty old when he was a cub, but she looked beautiful here. She looked a bit like Meg, in fact.

'What brings you here, though?' his Cub leader enquired of him. 'You don't go to this school, do you? I know you used to. But aren't you 40 years old now?'

'Well,' Iestyn replied, 'I just came to ask Mr Cash a question. You see, I think I've fallen asleep while driving on the motorway and I thought he might know what happens.'

'Because he died in a car crash in 1999?'

'Yes. Did you ever know him?'

'No, of course not. I was your Scout leader, not a teacher.'

'Oh yes, of course - you've probably never even been in this school. It hasn't changed a bit.'

Iestyn was going to say something about how you wouldn't get three bags of sweets for £1 these days, but he was halted abruptly by a blaring sound that filled the classroom and something like magnesium flashing across his vision.

'Ah,' Mrs Woodcock said, 'that must be the end of the lesson.'

thirteen

THE HARDEST THING TO SEE...

have got to the point finally when I need to write all this down. As a reflection I suppose, which seems to be the right word to use. I suspect nobody reading this will believe me, but I'm not writing this down to be believed. Just to give her a voice; if not a name.

It started on New Year's Eve just after my 18th birthday, which was in late November. It was my first year of legal drinking and so my mates and I had hit the festivities hard and had returned home completely hammered. I stood looking at myself in the full-length mirror that hung on my bedroom door, giggling at how funny I was, how clever to be off my face, before toppling into a chair as I tried to remove my trousers. Amid my drunken performance, it took me a few seconds to register how odd it seemed that my reflection was still standing upright in the mirror (the room was starting to spin at this point and my senses were all pulling together to prevent me from vomiting - something for which they were woefully unqualified). The reflection maintained his vigil of standing and observing. Drunk people find danger adrenalising rather than horrifying, and as I groped to my feet I gawped at the mirror not with fear, but rather with a studied fascination - as though I was watching film footage of a plane crash without being in one myself...though I have since revised that opinion. Doing my best to align my staggering self with its reflection, I reached out a hand to the glass. My reflection nodded chummily but didn't touch back.

I say it was my reflection. It was, and even then I knew it was 'me', but he was rounder than I was and had longer hair slicked back behind his ears.

'Say it, then,' he said.

'...Why am I so fat?'

'Mm-hm. That's what university does to you - and I mean to you specifically.'

What you need to understand is that I'd never been drunk before. I'd had a beer here and there, but the effects of ludicrous amounts of alcohol had never tormented me, and so I was ushering in all the side-effects - spinning rooms, blurred vision, visitations from my older self - with that sense of invulnerability that the inebriate possesses.

'Look, you're going to be sick in a minute, so just pay attention for a bit - we don't need to have a conversation, trust me.'

'OK,' I replied, with a moral fortitude that only gross intoxication offers.

'I don't know how any of this works,' he said. 'This is only my second time here and I wasn't sure whether anything would happen. But it has. I don't think we have very long, but this is a real thing.'

At this point in time the beer in my system fulfilled its oath and came racing with great haste and speed towards my mouth.

'Hang on…I'm coming back…'

'No, you're not!' he said with urgency. 'Stop a second…'

But some things in life are just unpreventable, and we don't always realise at the time those things which aren't. By the time I had finished vomiting my revelry down into the toilet and returned to the mirror, all I could see was a gaunt, saccharine version of my current self. At least I looked slim.

The following year I was nineteen and I was ready. I had drunk my way through most of the Home Counties during my first term at university, but I refused to go out on New Year's Eve - much to the suspicion of my flatmates. From 11pm I was standing by the mirror in my dorm room (the type or size of mirror never had any bearing) just waiting. During the intervening months and their more sober moments I had, at intervals, convinced myself that I had imagined the whole thing, but I could never quite shake the feeling that it had actually been real. As I waited impatiently, ready to label myself a lunatic and drown my gaslighting subconscious in vodka, I nevertheless had a clear plan: to pass on some information that hadn't been shared on the previous occasion. Maybe some key intel about the year I had just lived would galvanise my younger self into credulity. I would simply tell him that Arsenal had won the FA Cup.

At 11:45pm, as the pantomime of student drunkenness was entering its third act, something changed. My reflection in the mirror seemed to cloud over, as though a pipe smoking collective had infiltrated my living quarters. As the smoke cleared I could see myself from a year before, giggling and stumbling, in the bedroom of my parents house that was now, I knew, my Mum's art studio. When the moron in the mirror rose to his feet and reached out a hand, I was so caught up in the relief and excitement that I just waved back. (Remember, it was the first time for both of us in a sense). Unfortunately, the eighteen-year-old acted very much as before, racing to the toilet before I had chance to tell him anything. By the time he returned, the mirror had smoked out again...but I wasn't left alone. Staring back at me now was my twenty-year-old self, no slimmer, but wearing a look of determination.

'Hi!' I said.

'Hello. Listen, it's Crystal Palace.'

'Who won the...'

'...the FA Cup, yes. And watch out for the dog-walker at the zebra crossing on your driving test,' he said urgently. Just wait until she crosses, OK? Maybe you can avoid failing like I did.'

'How does this all work?' I asked.

'I don't know how or why, or whether we can change anything.'

'OK...OK, what else,' I stammered.

'Just remember those things. Let's just...'

Then he was gone. It had been less than a minute. But I had my two pieces of information. And now I had to wait once more.

Crystal Palace won the FA Cup that year. They started at odds of 44/1, which won me £440. I was reluctant to put any money down, in case the universe or God disqualified me - in case you weren't allowed to do that. But £10 didn't seem like a gratuitous bet to place - plus I was a student, who couldn't have drawn on treasure troves of cash even if he'd desired to.

74

I also took my driving test. I had just successfully completed a reverse around a corner and was heading back towards the test centre when I saw a woman walking her dog. She dallied at a zebra crossing, seemed to almost cross then turned obtusely away. I brought the car to a calm but deliberate halt.

'Is there a reason you've stopped?' the examiner asked me.

'I think she's going to cross and so I'm erring on the side of caution,' I replied.

Sure enough, as I said this the woman spun on her heel and stepped briskly into the road, waving her hand in thanks at the learner driver.

When the examiner told me back at the test centre that I had successfully passed my driving test, I was double-exhilarated. Not only did I now have the freedom of the roads but, less prosaically, I had changed the future of the universe in a tiny but decisive way.

You really have to have suckled voraciously at the teet of psychedelia to even begin conceptualising what that did to my mind. The sturdy equilibrius mind of the non-user shouldn't work too hard rummaging around in ramifications and paradoxes.

I spent the next week scratching thoughts and questions onto a notepad like a manic detective. I didn't know how much time 'we' would have the following New Year's Eve - or even if it would happen again, although I suspected this was my life now - and I was fairly keen to glean some more betting tips. I was hoping my future self would know that.

The first thing 21 said to me was: 'You changed it.'

'I did? So you never failed your driving test?'

'I did both. I remember both.' He looked as confused as I felt, but there wasn't time. I held up the jotter in my hand.

'Excellent, I hoped you might do that. Man City for the FA Cup,' he said. 'And they win the league, too.'

'Great…wait, they do? Bollocks.'

'And Real Madrid win the Champions League, and Pirate Boy wins the Grand National, OK? Pirate…Boy.'

'Got it, I said.' 'Anything else…?' But no; the future was again a thing of memory. *Alterable* memory.

The next year, my final one at university, I made £23,000. The following year I made nearly double that, and by the time I was twenty four I owned a house outright. It was only an end-terrace, but next to my friends I was Nebuchadnezzar. I always used a different bookmaker for the wagers and had various bank accounts. In addition, I had a lot of money stashed in my house, which even regular debauched nights out and perennial takeaways did little to chip away at.

The precise timespan of the interactions was never an exact science (and how science has any bearing on this whole saga, or vice versa, I gave up trying to evaluate a long time ago - and I assume the other timelines did too). Usually we would have around thirty seconds, but sometimes it was closer to a minute. So we would always start with the money-making and then, if there was time, shunt to other topics, which might be something like 'Don't kiss Cheryl' or 'Russia's started another war' or 'You call her Daisy.' Daisy was a cat as it turned out. But always we would start with the money. Either way, there's only so much you can change. Prior to that conversation I would have passed on the same basic hustling spiel to my younger self, although I never included the personal addendums - for some reason I just didn't want to live in that distorted reality of the 'yes it happened' and the 'no it didn't'. I was happy enough with my lot, and my younger self would be happy with his (mine).

'What do you mean you remember both?' I asked one year - although I can't remember which - after the serious business had been concluded. 'How can you remember two things happening when it was the same event twice?' Neither *he* nor I had any idea how it worked, and even if we'd had an hour to unpack it I suspect it would have made little sense to me. All FutureMe could ever say was that both things happened, only one lasted. Each year, the day after the FA Cup Final or the Superbowl or whatever, money would suddenly appear in his bank account. That sort of non-corporeal manifestation didn't addle our brains too much, but it got more complex with other scenarios: when a friend my future self had fallen out with 9 months prior would suddenly get in touch in early January as though nothing had happened; or when a neighbour didn't in fact die and that Irish family never moved in next door. If my older self had given me the hint, I would often be able to circumvent the disaster - occasionally leaving him with a new problem! Sometime in his late twenties - although not in mine - he had to explain to his fiancee why another woman was claiming to be his current girlfriend and asking why he had abruptly ghosted her? I don't know how he wriggled out of that, but we laughed together about it, and I always reaped the dividend the second time round.

He was my hero, my Minuteman, the pioneer and perfecter of my wealth, and each meeting was like stumbling into King Solomon's Mines to prostrate myself before the increasingly decadent surroundings through the looking glass - the certain prophecy of things not seen, the now but not yet.

Mirror, mirror, on the wall, who's the jammiest of them all?

Then when I was thirty three years old and newly married, my future self shuffled the pack. He informed me, with my head down and my pen poised to sign my next life-warrant: 'Your daughter is born with down-syndrome.' I raised my eyes to meet his and saw that he looked grave and tired and, for the first time ever, skinnier than me - but not impressively so. His experience had taken the laughter lines around my eyes and manhandled them into wrinkles.

'Just be aware,' he said. 'I don't want you to panic in front of Janey like I did.'

We weren't expecting a child at that point, although Janey had been making her intentions very clear and I was warming to the idea. After all, I had no career to preserve and the belt-tightening rigmarole with which most new parents have to contend wouldn't darken our door.

'Thanks for telling me,' I said. I could see tears in his eyes. It didn't seem appropriate to talk about how to shaft the sports betting system after that, although I did ask about the World Cup. I don't know that we said very much at all apart from that. I think I told him he looked thin.

I wore a condom for the next nine months. Janey was upset with me, but I told her I just wanted the timing to be perfect. We would have the rest of our lives to be parents, I told her.

On New Year's Eve I started proceedings by advising my younger self to keep his breaches buckled - the first time I'd ever disclosed any moral advice. He shrugged and smiled. He didn't mention that I looked thin, but why would he? I didn't.

As the dependable chirpiness of past reflection smoked out and the window to the future opened up as usual, I found myself looking into the eyes of a man I didn't recognise at all.

'You selfish prick,' he said, softly at first.

'What's that, mate?'

'You selfish F*****G prick, you killed my little girl!'

If he had looked slim the previous year, now he was emaciated; ghostly.

'I didn't,' I protested, thrown by the employment of a word I had never used; suddenly terrified by my own reflection. 'I was just waiting so that when she was born she would be healthy. I thought…'

'Are you f****** mad?!' he screamed back at me. 'You don't put an order in for a baby! You killed my tiny girl, you stupid f****** selfish c***!'

Like a bridge collapsing on top of me, I recognised that I had failed to read the room the previous year. How was that conceivable? How had I misread my own room? I was *him*, wasn't I? He was *me*.

'I'll change it then,' I flustered, mindlessly. But he was gone. The reflection was still visible but he had left the room. The treasure trove was empty.

And I wouldn't change it, would I, after all? I had already spoken to my past self and had blithely offered my air-headed counsel. The bridge had collapsed.

Janey and I tried to get pregnant the following year, but with no luck. All the money in the world can't create that sort of life.

Chris (as I started to think of him after that) didn't talk to me for another five years. At each year's end I would stand pleadingly by the mirror and try to communicate with him, to say sorry and ask for help. He would always be there, visible, but he remained silent, occasionally meeting my stare for a second with a look of such utter malice that I've never seen in another human being. He didn't tell me when the housing market crashed, or when Janey, childless and broken, left me for a coworker.

I said none of this to my younger self who, year on year, flourished and thrived and carried himself with a lightness I no longer had. I was working hard not to hate him; to not simply bite along the food chain. But he wasn't me. Neither of them were me. The whole thing had fractured.

I am almost finished now. Finally, last year, six years after the outburst, Chris was standing there waiting for me.

'Make sure you say goodbye to Dad,' he said flatly. At that, he took a towel and was preparing to hang it over the mirror.

'Wait…please,' I said desperately. He lowered the towel but didn't look at me.

'…How's Cassie?' I asked. My wife - second wife - had been struggling with chest palpitations all year, and so I was tentatively asking for an update in case I could help where the medical world was floundering.

'I don't know who that is,' he said, without recognition or emotion, and then the towel covered the mirror.

I swung away from the mirror as though turned around by some unseen current. How could he not know Cassie? We had been together for three years, married for two. How could he not know her?

But it wasn't that hard to work out. Not when you stop to consider someone other than yourself. For amid all the brain-numbing paradox and pantomime, one thing was as clear as polished glass: that man who used to be me was stuck in a future he didn't create and didn't choose. Where I had moved on, he had been unable to. Maybe he had met Cassie; maybe he hadn't even gone that far. But we were very different people, he and I. Different species, even; kept apart by an inch of glass like animals in a reptile house. He was much older than I was. Grief had taken him to places I had never had to go, although I may yet. I don't know what the future holds, you see.

There's a saying in a book, or a film or something, that says: 'Only death can pay for life.' Chris' death - his grief - had paid for my life. But it wasn't willingly given. He hadn't offered it up; I stole it. And in turn, my life had paid for his death. And I didn't even know my daughter's name.

I have got to the point finally when I need to write all this down, as a reflection. For it is December 31st and I have just looked into the mirror: into an empty room with the curtains taken down and the carpets bare. And for the first time in years I can see myself as I actually am.

But I don't know how to change it.

Part 3:
DAWN

fourteen

NOTHING LIKE REDEMPTION

From the diary of Mr. A. Morgan, esq.
Heartlands, Hanover County,
September 1899

I rode into Valentine at dawn as the townsfolk were rising and the hubbub of cattle and carpentry began, as it always did without fail, once the first light of day shone forth over the uppermost ridge of the Grizzlies. I had spent the last couple of nights camping up in North Ambarino, around Calumet Ravine but had tacked off east to avoid the Watiti tribe whom I do not trust, and the soldiers garrisoned at Fort Wallace, who do not trust me.

Ain't no mystery being up so far north in those mountains. I had been on the trail of a certain bear, of legendary stature and disposition, whom it had served my interest to hunt and kill - something I had managed successfully at the second attempt, and I do not wish to speak of the first attempt at this time. The crusted fur hide of my aggressor now lay rolled and tied on the back of Beulah, who I do not believe was much obliged to be carrying his present cargo. A couple of wild carrots and a sprig of mint from my satchel soon settled him down right enough. Following the line of the railroad tracks from Bacchus station over to the Brandywine Drop, I turned, real southern like, and headed thereafter down into the Roanoke Valley and along the Kamassa river, thinking I might stop to fish a while as the heat of the day was upon me.

My first duty upon riding into Valentine was to visit the butcher, who seems, by all accounts, to maintain a perennially open stall, even on the sabbath. I traded into his keeping a brace of rabbit pelts and a deer hide, lightening Beulah's load ever so slightly, but not to the point at which he seemed grateful. The bear skin I was saving until I could locate a Canadian trapper who seems to appear, as if by magic, when I am out in the wilderness minding my own business.

It was hanging day in Valentine, and quite a crowd was a-massing to enjoy the spectacle. For my part, I do not consider death a leisure pursuit; it is rather, in my line of work, a grim but necessary consequence of my trade, within which I have grown in reputation and repute on account of my not yet being dead.

My second duty of business in the mud-caked, bang-and-crash of Valentine was to have a drink, mayhaps several drinks. My financial situation is currently rosey, on account of having found, after some help from God and those outside the state line, a gold bar, pretty as a peach, spared from the flames in the hellish and fire-scorched town of Limpenny; or, I should say, the former town, for there is no human life there now, if ever there was. Having been, over what seems like days but may actually be months, faced with spawns of Satan's own bodyguard - mauled by a grizzly, stalked by a cougar and ridden right into the jaws of a gator in its Bayou hideout - I considered the tithing of my divine inheritance into sipping whiskey something of a sound investiture.

A number of the O'Driscoll boys have been spotted hanging their sorry assess out around the town, and whilst I do enjoy cowhiding those spit-lipped Irish vagrants, I did not wish to add a second public hanging to the day's roster, as surely as pumpkins ain't cabbages. I thereby, with all grace and gentility, kept my Schofield revolver asleep in its holster as I set up camp at the saloon bar. The piano was a-playing and the barman was a-whistling, and I do most enjoy that sense of conviviality.

How long have I been here? I do not know. Dutch and the rest of the gang will be hitched around Clemens Point or Shady Belle, I do not doubt, and I cannot stay here, in this chair, forever. I am an outlaw, constantly on the run. What exactly I am running from or running towards, I do not have the wisdom to know, nor the words to convey. I do what I need to do every day just to survive.

I know that I must leave this place, but I am afraid, because I do not know what is beyond the horizon or what the future holds. Outside this country is a whole world which frightens me. Here I feel safe, I feel somehow invincible. My life is meaningful here. Here I am able to save what I have lost; I have myriad chances to redeem. I do not have the skills to survive in that other world. I do not know how to love, for I have loved only myself.

I heard a reverend once say…it may have been Reverend Strauss but I think somehow it belongs to another time, maybe a past life…that The Lord in his heaven delights in three things: to reveal, to reverse and to restore. I believe in the God of this world that I know, where I move and have my being. As for the God outside this map, I do not know what I think about him. Does he even know I am here? If he walked into this saloon bar in the town of Valentine and saw an unshaven and weather-beaten man sipping whiskey at the bar, with beaver chaps and a panther-skin waistcoat so dearly bought, would he know my name? My…real name? Does he know that I made the wrong choice; that I was selfish and scared and that I lost that which was most dear? Is he able to change that somehow…to rewrite it? I ain't scared of dying young, what frightens me is living wrong.

My third and my final reason for being here in Valentine is Mary. I know she is within spitting distance of where I now sit. I am here for her. I have come back here for her. But I have not seen her for so long, and I do not know what to say to her. I am not good at explaining with words; I make myself clear only when I explain with gunpowder.

The sun is setting outside with great haste, sinking like my heart, setting on the things I wish I had done. I will take a room here, take a bath, and in the morning I shall visit Mary Linton and I shall hope to tell her everything. Courage, a man once said, is being scared and saddling up anyway.

After that, I will ride south on Beulah. I am sure I can find work and adventure that will keep me occupied for another day. Another man once said that there is no better place to heal a broken heart than on the back of a horse. I think about that a lot. I almost always conclude that, in saying that, he was wrong.

He was very wrong.

fifteen

CLEAR UP ON AISLE 3

t was thirteen days after my Grandmother's funeral and I had laid to rest the guilt of not being there to say goodbye when she died. As I rationalised it, I had already grieved over her; she'd been ill for some time and the spritely pensioner with the almost pantomime supply of treats had been supplanted by a sagging crinkle-cut imitation of my Nanny. It wasn't really her for the last few years, I had convinced myself. She'd had a good innings, as some people say - although she had never liked cricket so I don't know why that was the best analogy. 'She'd solved more than her fair share of Countdown Conundrums' would be apter.

I hadn't been to see her before I flew out to Crete with the rugby lads. No, I hadn't done that and I wish that I had. On reflection, I had made the mistake of normalising her illness, lapsing into the illogical belief that, because she'd survived infirmity for so long, perhaps she would never die. Old people can seem so frail and simultaneously immortal, having lived for so long and through so many trials. But the phone call I got while cruising the Malia strip swiftly disabused me of that fallacy.

But I had dealt with it, and nothing could have been further from my thoughts as I recipe-hunted around *Asda* that afternoon. I had decided to make pulled pork, something I always did to impress people I was trying to impress. I had someone to impress that evening and I was keen to make a good second impression. On date number one I had drunk a bit too much and then spoken in a

Russian accent for large parts of the evening. The fact she was coming round at all hinted at some low self-esteem issues on her part, but it was always nice to be afforded a chance at redemption. I would wheel out my masterpiece and hope that dessert might not be culinary. I had a pack of *After Eights* in the trolley, if not.

I often boast (and did, I think numerous times, on date one) that I make the finest pulled pork in Western Europe, and that the existence of a Budapestian crone was the only thing stopping me from having full dominion over the whole continent. Like I say, I had drunk quite a lot. I mean, I do make nice pulled pork, but I found the recipe in a *Morrison's* quarterly so it's not quite the secret family recipe I'd led her to believe. What's worse, I never used quite the same mixture for the homemade BBQ sauce, and so I was rooting through the parade of spices when I saw my dead Grandmother coming down the aisle towards me.

It wasn't her, of course - this isn't some creepy Stephen King book that stops you sleeping at night. The person making a slow, ponderous scouring of the aisle was not Dorothy Rowlton of 110 Hurdis Road. But I saw her: same greying perm; same all-purpose, all-weather, all-decades coat of the same nondescript brown that made an entire generation of women invisible - a generation which hadn't quite recovered from shouts of lights out and remained wary of anything too bright. The old lady made her way down the aisle towards me pushing a trolley full of memories, and suddenly I wasn't in the Stafford branch of *Asda* - I was in 1990 and we were walking along Shirley High Street together. I had been telling her about *Subbuteo* and how I never played by the rules, and I was the second best player in the school football team but Gareth was better although I was slightly faster.

We went into *Iceland* and bought choc ices and mixed veg and one of everything else. I hadn't asked for choc ices but I did want some and she knew that - and besides, she had worked hard all her life and if the reward for that was buying your grandson choc ices because he was staying with you, then boo sucks to everything else.

Up and down the aisles we went with me pushing the trolley, 'but let me know if it gets too heavy and I'll take over, love'. I was only staying for four nights, but by the time we got to the checkout the trolley looked like it had ram-raided a Quarter-Master's storehouse.

'Well, you won't go hungry, Dorothy,' the cashier said. 'And who's this young man?'

'My eldest grandson. He's staying for a few days.'

'Oh, how lovely. And what are you going to be doing?'

'Well, lots of fun things. He can start by putting these into his sticker album.' At this, she picked up a large indiscriminate handful of packets from the 'Impulse Buy' section and loaded them onto the conveyor belt. The *Italia '90* World Cup was about to start and I had been avidly trying to fill the whole *Panini* album. I would eventually succeed with the help of a few cheeky postal orders, but it would be the last time I even came close to filling one of those things. I've had a soft spot for Czechoslovakia's Tomas Schurarvy ever since.

'You're a lucky boy then, aren't you?' the cashier said as she scanned a tub of hummus - although that must be where the memory tapers because I don't think British supermarkets stocked hummus in 1990, and Nanny certainly wouldn't have wanted them to.

The memory melted away like a choc ice left on a bench. My muscle memory spasmed me back to the present, but I kept my vigil there at the end of the aisle as the old lady made her ponderous way towards me, trolley wheels and hips fighting it out for who could creek the loudest. When she reached me, she stopped and looked up.

'Excuse me, can you move, I'm trying to get past.'

I hesitated through slight perplexity - she'd never been one to get irritated.

'Excuse me, can you move please, I want to get past you,' my dead Grandmother chided me - before reality fully undistorted itself and I found myself gazing curiously at a random old woman.

'Sorry...sorry, yes,' I said. She gave me a suspicious look.

'Do you need any help with your trolley?' I asked.

'I don't need any help. If I need help I'll ask someone who works here, thank you. You're still in the way.'

I stepped aside and the stoic Captain sailed her wobbly vessel onwards.

I saw her in the frozen goods aisle next. I had swept a load of herb jars into my trolley to randomise the pork seasoning, and had decided to pick up a pack of choc ices in case the *After Eights* made me look cheap and only interested in sex. The old lady who wasn't my dead grandmother was placing a tub of Neapolitan ice cream into a premeditated spot on the trolley floor.

'Have you ever had these choc ices?' I enquired of her, holding up the box.

'No, I haven't. Far too messy on your hands. And why do you keep talking to me? I'm in rather a hurry and I don't have time.'

The old lady checked her list, ticked off the ice-cream, and rolled on with purpose. She clearly had a defined route and a pre-ordained shopping list. There would be no impulse buys.

I skirted round the other aisles for a few extra accoutrements for my soirée - a scented candle, nice bread, three different flavours of air-freshener. My intention was to turn my second floor flat behind the Masonic Lodge into a feast for all the senses in the way that I imagine a Sultan might do. I found a free checkout and started hoarding my items through customs, scowling at the checkout girl who smirked at the extraordinary abundance of air-fresheners.

As I was preparing to pay, thinking how long this had taken and how I would now have very little time to make the toilet smell like field after field of lavender, the greys and browns of the old lady shunted into dock at the next checkout. She looked across at me and I smiled, and she frowned and began unloading her goods.

'Get everything you need, did you, Jane?' the man at the next checkout asked her.

'Yes, I think so, I'll just get my purse...Oh, and a packet of those football stickers please, love - my grandson collects them.'

'Are you collecting points?' the smug girl at my checkout asked me.

'Sorry, what?'

'Reward points - are you collecting them?'

'Erm...no, no. No, I'm not.'

'You're all done then. Have a good night.'

I lumbered my burdensome bags-for-life towards the supermarket exit, that thin threshold between two worlds. The washed-out light of evening had covered the tarmac of the Stafford *Asda* and I would definitely now be late for my date. I turned and walked back towards the row of checkouts. The cantankerous old lady's spring-loaded holdall had been erected, and she was readying herself for her journey onwards. She looked up at my approach.

'It was nice to meet you,' I said. 'I hope to bump into you again somewhere.'

She tilted her head at me with a look of curious sympathy, but she nodded.

'Goodbye, love,' my Grandmother said.

sixteen

THAT SUNDAY
I WENT TO CHURCH

Sunday 12th

To say that I'm only a hatches, matches and dispatches guy wouldn't be quite true. I'm not an atheist. There was a week back in 2009 when I had terrible food poisoning from some kebabs and decided that God couldn't be real, but that belief left me as prosaically as salmonella passes out of the body. Nor, though, would it be true to claim that I'm particularly religious - and I'm not even sure what people mean when they say that. Does it simply mean believing in God, or going to church every week? Pretty sure those two aren't a direct overlap in a Venn diagram.

The best way to describe my current state is that I feel 'spiritually haunted'. Not in a scary way; I just can't shake the feeling - the creeping feeling - that something or someone is out there trying to get my attention. I honestly don't know which of the many Gods or Goddesses, if any, is responsible for this phenomenon, and it worries me that there seems to be so little convergence of beliefs between the Big 6. But you have to start somewhere and I've got this hauntedness and I'm starting with that.

So today I went to church. Maybe next week I'll go to synagogue or a mosque, but today I went to church because that's the religion

I'm most familiar and (probably, to be honest) most comfortable with. I didn't research any churches beforehand, nor did I pick one at random or have one appear to me in a dream. My selection process was more banal, in that every day on my bus into the city I pass an elegantly brutish church in Stoke Newington, sitting noble and belligerent against a tide of encroaching modernity. It looks lived-in and solvent, not draughty and desolate, and so that's where I went. The sign at the entrance displayed the service start-time as 10:30am, so I left Manor House at 9:00 and took a leisurely constitutional in my Sunday best (which is a hoodie and a pair of jeans with holes round the hem because I got 'long' instead of regular).

St Mary's is an Anglican church, so although I'm not a season-ticket holder at these events I've been to enough school Christmas concerts to avoid feeling overawed. I thought, maybe a bit harshly, that I could probably avoid the happy-clappy, overly-effusive smiles and limp handshakes of the born-again tribe by selecting a Church of England - although I didn't know what to expect by way of welcome or attendance: was this a Premier League church which sold out every match, or were they languishing in the lower leagues? Would I be able to buy a half-time hot dog, or was it just weak tea in the shower afterwards? For certain, my football analogy had taken an odd turn and needed subbing off.

I made my way up the drive and a steady throng joined me and absorbed me into its warm huddly embrace. Good numbers, then - at least a Championship outfit. A woman with Trebor-white hair on the door handed me a programme, and with my football analogy now bouncing back after injury I only just avoided handing her a couple of quid.

Inside the church there was a large lobby/foyer thing, where people lucky enough to know each other were chortling and ho-humming depending on the conversation they were having. I melted through into the main…dome? Theatre? The bit where they do the church, anyway.

The seating was all pews - so many of them - but restored and varnished so the place looked like a wholesaler for microbrewery furnishings. I took a seat about two thirds back on the far end of a row, overlooked by a stained-glass window of someone dying - that really got me in the mood, obviously. A kneeling cushion, like a miniature punch bag in evening attire, hung flaccidly in front of me. I sat on my phone for a minute to shield myself from curious looks, then worried that being on my phone might be precisely the thing to attract attention, a handheld supercomputer dwarfed by archaic pillars and ancient rafters. I was starting to wonder which was the greater anachronism, me or Christianity, when a long-limbed man who looked like an off-duty wizard shuffled into the row next to me with his wife, who was ostensibly a shrew in human fancy dress. She smiled a mousey smile that fell somewhere between conciliatory and anguished, while he bowed to me like a tilting lance, his spine making the sound of a crumbling aspirin as he did so.

The rest of the chortlers and ho-hummers eventually seeped through from the foyer/lobby and took up practised residence along predestined rows. The organ pipes cleared their throats and, in telepathic unity, the gathered mass rose in a near-simultaneous movement like an under-choreographed Mexican wave, and two hymns were sung, mouthed, whispered, adhered to, depending on musical adeptness or level of interest. One I knew, the one about how great God art, and the other I didn't, but I didn't feel like I was missing out by never having heard it. I wasn't going to go straight home and Spotify the s*** out of it.

Nobody seemed to be really getting into the music that much (and in fairness to the happy-clappers who I was mercilessly denigrating just now, they at least seem to have chosen their own playlist). The notable and startling exception to the no-fun rule was a girl four rows forward - I guess she was early twenties - who was having an absolute bop, waving her arms and saying 'Yeeeeaaaaahhhh'. Perhaps she had her airpods in and was attending her own silent disco, or maybe she just meant the words she was singing. Set against the perfectly manicured rows of straight-backed reverence, her joyous and chaotic movement looked like a protest. She was a blackbird who'd flown into an examination hall; a one-woman flashmob who went ahead even when nobody else showed up; as anomalous as a man in a hoodie checking *Tinder* under godly arches.

The second hymn ended, or at least the organist abruptly ceased playing, had perhaps died, and then the reverend took centre stage, using the last few strangled notes from the organ pipes as his walk-on music. The priest was younger and more handsome than I would have imagined, but he was dressed like a caricature of a satire on a misheard joke. It would help the church's stance against gay marriage if a lot of their top boys didn't flounce around in ball gowns. I almost snorted at my own private joke and had to turn it into a cough to cover my tracks. (Nb. This life-hack also works with loud farts).

Reverend Handsome spoke for a while from a million miles away, his reedy voice unaided - although I'm sure he thought it was - by diction taken straight from Amateur Dramatics 101. Nobody talks like this, I thought - and I'm right about that. I'm sure he's clever and earnest and *insert virtue-signalling caveats here*, but his whole vibe was that of a street performer dressed for a kinky fancy dress party - and I'm not modelling my life philosophy on that, thanks everso.

'Get off and bring on the silver-painted statue guy who also robot dances for some reason,' I was surprised nobody shouted. But I'd seen enough. I resolved to leave during the next dirge - I had shown up and it was all very quaint and ceremonial, but me and this church were non-overlapping Venn diagrams. It said nothing to me about my life, as someone once sung and I genuinely don't know who…The Clash? The Smiths?

I had zoned out and was brought startlingly to task by a sudden collective fidgeting. 'Let us offer once another a sign of peace,' the vicar said, and all of a sudden people were shimmying and swerving and grabbing at one another across varnished pine.

'Peace be with you,' the wizard said, reaching across an elongated hand. I furtively offered my own hand, like that guy on the roof of the Sistine Chapel, and replied with 'Also with you'. Miraculously, this seemed to be the correct response and I was offered peace by several people I'll never see in my life again, starting to enjoy it while wondering what any of this ritual would mean in a real conflict situation. After three or four handshakes, I was really growing in confidence with my 'Peace be with you' spiel and was slightly crestfallen to find that we were now going to clamour another hymn. I got in a final handshake after the bell, so to speak, and iced it on top with a resounding 'All the best'. Then, as planned, I turned to slip out of the pew - but was blocked by a big toothy smile and a loud 'May the force be with you' from the dancing girl.

'And also with you,' I said, and found myself chuckling at the shameless unfettered happiness of my interlocutor.

'I am your Father!' she said sternly, as tremulous lead pipes once more led the people on a hypnotic journey towards mass forgetfulness.

The girl didn't move; in fact, she stood next to me, turned to face the front and once again began dancing, unsynchronised, incongruous and majestic. By verse three of a song which must surely have been titled 'Hosanna', I was swaying along with her, a late and under-prepared arrival to her flashmob. Her voice was never going to garner her any prizes, but she knew the words. She knew them off by heart and, it was clear from her wide-eyed frivolity, she meant every one of them. Towards the end of the song she held my hand, and she meant that too.

The organ gave up the ghost and the crowd settled itself decorously once more into its collective seat.

'That was fun!' my new friend declared, and her audacity yanked a guffaw out of me that I didn't even try to cover with a cough. 'Bye!' she said to me as she skipped the short distance back to where her parents were looking with benign surveillance.

And then it was the end of the service and the sexy vicar left, the choir stumbling after him like a parade of ambivalent cadavers, and some people bowed their heads for a while and some people busied themselves with their hymn books - seemingly nobody wanting to give the appearance of making a quick getaway. And my friend bounced past, waving at me with the sort of wave you only really need to attract the attention of someone on the other side of a large car park. And her mother leaned into to me with a slightly guarded coyness and said, 'Sorry about that, she has some additional needs.' Quite aware that there are more bad responses than good ones to a statement like that, I simply feathered my hands outwards in a non-threatening manner which I think worked well within that environment. And then I got in line and trudged my way out of there, meeting people's pencil-thin smiles with my own, not being greeted or bidden or offered anything by way of beverage. And I joined Jonny and Greg at the pub and we got slowly hammered in the afternoon sun on benches that looked like church pews.

And I thought about that young girl with additional needs. Who had difficulty learning that you don't just go up and talk to lonely people in church; that you don't dance and sing when the news is clearly so severe, as though really it might be good news. Who held my hand when I needed it.

That girl wasn't the only one with additional needs. I know *I* have. I need to find my way home. I need to chase that ghost, this haunted feeling, through the woods and along the valleys and up to the mountain tops. And that girl, whose name I don't know - St. Mary I'll call her - she made me feel like my needs were special, in that cold but strangely warm place.

'I am your Father,' she had said.
And I'm smiling again.

seventeen

HARRY'S PIGEONS

The day the pigeons didn't fly away from Harry came as a surprise, and he wasn't really one for surprises these days. The older you get, the population share of pleasant surprises drops significantly per capita.

The pigeons were his friends, of course. They always flocked to his garden of a morning as the sun stepped briskly over the horizon, knowing full well that the six bird feeders would have been replenished during the night, and that seeds and mealworm and waxworms and those peanuts they all obsessed over would be on offer: a breakfast buffet fit for kings and winged rodents alike. Here they would congregate daily, bowing and scraping and pecking at the feet of the monolithic feeders, nature's worshippers making their druidic pilgrimage.

The pigeons knew where to come, through instinct or muscle memory or committee meeting or something, and they recognised Harry, but they never stayed when the lock to the back door scratched in its rusty housing and the post-war lean-to shivered open. Whatever primal law of attraction the feeders possessed, it played second fiddle to that even more ancient, always ultimately thwarted, desire to stay alive. The pigeons never fought like foxes or froze like rabbits; they always flew.

Harry liked to think that the pigeons were just being respectful, livery servants making themselves scarce once the Emperor rose for his morning constitutional; or devout churchgoers, parting reverentially as the God-presence passed through their ranks. But really they were just birds - scavenous, self-interested birds. They came for the meal and left before the speeches. If there was free food on offer then you could guarantee their presence, but they never just popped in. Harry knew humans like that, too; but humans should know better, he thought.

So the day the pigeons didn't flee, even after Harry's slippered feet dudded and papped against the patio slabs, came as a welcome surprise. Maybe it was because the door was already open and they hadn't heard the scraping of the key or the shaking of the lean-to. Maybe they just desired an audience with the Emperor.

'Nice and easy, friends, nice and easy. It's just me, Harry, your humble servant...your generous liege lord.'

Taking a scuffed tin from his cardigan pocket and a wooden pipe from where it had been left negligently overnight on the wall, Harry filled the bowl with a generous pinch of *Spirit of Scotland*. His wife would have told him off for smoking so close to the house, but bereavement came with very few dividends and this was his full share. He clicked his calloused thumb tip down on the lighter, but it wouldn't catch. It was old, like him, and often needed topping up, like him. The pigeons were still hanging about, swanning around in the early light which had a sickly washed-out look to it this morning. The sun had clearly got his hat on, but perhaps he wasn't able to come out to play just yet.

Slowly, cautiously, Harry hoisted himself up the three steps from the newly-weeded patio, past the fallen statue and onto the path of bark chippings that curved across the lawn. A solitary pigeon, an outlier from the main party, was pecking happily away at the cropped turf, pewter-tinged tail feathers up.

'Don't mind me, friend, I'm just catching my breath. You carry on with your party.'

When Harry and his wife had bought the house back in whenever it was, those steps could be bested in a single bound. Now it was like climbing Jacob's Ladder outside Edale. A young man had visited the other day to offer a quote on replacing the steps with a ramp, and maybe Harry would consider that at some point.

'1978, that was it,' Harry told the pigeon. 'The year before Joanna was born.' He rammed his stick into the bark chippings to mark this victory of memory. Something still worked, at least.

Harry's breath took longer and longer to refill these days - a slow puncture without a repair kit - but he mustered enough energy for the second leg of this morning relay: a gentle riverside walk to the pagoda. The curve of the path was modelled purposely on the shape of the Thames. It would have been quicker and easier to lay a straight track, but for Harry the daily tracing of that sinuous bark waterway always felt like an achievement, the completion of something, but more than that: a memory of a former life; a home he no longer had reason or means to visit.

A dishevelled pigeon was fording the river at Gravesend, but Harry took the bend at Greenwich from where he could see over into next door's garden. It had been so charming when Albert and Dawn lived there, before they both died there, but their children had turned it into student accommodation and now the garden looked bereft and unloved, neglected by a group of noisome young chaps who Harry thought needed less turbo injection and more muffler. As if to vindicate his own point, shouts of 'Oh God! Oh my God!' were coming from an open upstairs window. Harry was sure they were all perfectly nice young men, but he wouldn't recognise any of them if he passed them on the street.

'Woolwich...Dartford...here we are,' Harry said, reaching the estuary of the river path and stepping under the covered pagoda where two seats, one dull-bottomed and faded, one glossy and immaculate, waited for company. Here he would sit until Gill the cleaner arrived. The mock-Chinese structure was too ornate and showy for Harry's liking and he would have been happy enough with a shed, but his wife had wanted to use her retirement bonus on it and Harry had huffed about it but eventually conceded. There were exotic trinkets all over the garden: Grecian urns and Sicilian sickles and Hungarian milkweed and the fallen statue. None of them had been Harry's choice. He often struggled to remember where these items had come from, and sometimes it seemed that they had just appeared overnight, but he suspected it was down to his staccato memory rather than some intricate prank from the chaps next door.

Suddenly the pigeons bolted. In one chaotic and panicked murmuration, scores of wings stretched presaging shadows across the lawn as the whole flock fled the scene. Cupping his hand over his eyes, Harry looked heavenward to see the baleful outline of a peregrine falcon patrolling overhead, the angel of death for any member of the school caught not paying enough attention in class.

'Not today, thank you,' Harry said with an impotent swat of his hands. 'Clear off or I'll clip your wings!'

The falcon, its eyes waxing deadly and chill, passed on unseeing.

Harry leaned back on the lacquered pine without it creaking and had another fruitless try at resuscitating his pipe lighter. The sound of distant sirens fractured the peacefulness of the morning and he was hoping Gill was all right and hadn't been caught up in anything...when the pigeons returned en masse to the garden. Had they discerned that the coast was clear of doom-bringers, or had they resolved, like plucky revolutionaries, to make a stand, to dance out of step to the music of their DNA?

A large blustering bird, naped in royal green and half-collared with priestly white, settled with surprising grace onto the empty seat next to Harry. He stiffened up like a statue, worried that any movement might send the bird into retreat.

'I don't think I've seen you before, my dear,' Harry whispered. 'But you're very welcome here.' The pigeon must have been cultivated as a homer or something, unfazed as it was by immanent human presence. Tremulously, Harry reached out a hand to touch the bird, a Sistine Chapel reenactment where the incarnation was ornithological rather than theological. He felt the soft tickle of feathers on his fingertips and smiled at the touch, at how amenable to intimacy the pigeon appeared.

'You are a beauty, aren't you? Shall we stay here a little while and I can stroke your hair? And I could protect you from that hawk. Would you like that?'

The pigeon shuffled from foot to foot and Harry left his fingers to filter through the softness of mutual caress.

When Harry looked up a minute later, a tall lady in a smoke-grey cardigan was standing at the door to the lean-to, holding a key. He had been expecting Gill.

'This garden is lovely,' she said with a voice as soft as feathers.

'Yes, I look after it myself,' Harry said. 'Although the pigeons usually fly away.'

'I know,' the tall lady smiled. 'I wanted you to have a chance to say goodbye to your friends.'

'Why, where are we going?' Harry asked. 'Gill's coming.'

Now the lady chuckled. 'It takes a while to understand. But I am taking you to another garden.'

'But who will take care of my friends?'

'Don't worry, Harold. Not one of them is overlooked.'

Harry shrugged, raised himself from his bench and waded through the waters of the Thames, through the ranks of reverential pigeons, down the steps that needed a ramp - and towards his wife.

'Should I leave a note for Gill?' he asked. 'I'm not sure why she isn't here.'

'Gill will know where you've gone.' The lady opened her palm in the direction of the fallen statue. Harry looked down at it and saw that it was not actually a statue at all. He studied it with curiosity, realisation stroking his conscience with a soft hand. The touch of his wife's fingertips against his forearm ushered his focus away from the patio. Harry looked at her and a smile slowly flooded his face. 'That's the cardigan you died in,' he said.

'Yes.'

He studied her face as one studies a work of abstract art. 'You were so much older then.'

'Yes, I was, wasn't I. I wore this because I wanted you to recognise me.'

Now it was Harry's turn to chuckle.

'Oh, I would recognise *you* anywhere, young lady,' he said. 'I would recognise you anywhere.'

eighteen

AROMA

Geraldine always used her full name. She was never Geri or Jezz or Deeney. She always went by Geraldine because that's what her mother had named her and what her mother still called her when she could remember that Geraldine wasn't a day-nurse or an angel come to take her to heaven. Religious people do seem obsessed with angels taking them to heaven.

Geraldine lived - always had - with her mother. She had flirted with the idea of going to university, but she wasn't good at flirting and she had heard from a cousin that 78% of university is flirting. Geraldine couldn't remember whether the other 22% had been accounted for, but she decided anyhow that she would miss her mother too much if she went away and that wouldn't be fair. 'You'll find a job in the typing pool, I'm sure, clever girl like you,' her mum had said in 2002 when typewriters were already museum pieces.

'I think it's all computers now, Mum.'

'Aye, well, these things are sent to test us,' her mum had said.

Geraldine worked in an office with a group of other ladies and a young man who didn't want to be there. Their job was to sell advertising space in *Staffordshire Quarterly*, one of those local magazines that get pushed through people's doors and mainly advertise salons and independent butchers but occasionally will have an interview with Anthea Turner or Eddie Hall. 'Although I don't live in Staffs anymore,' they would always say, 'I still have fond memories of growing up there.'

Geraldine's job was to ring up these salons, independent butchers, beer wholesalers etc., and ask if they'd like to have a quarter page ad in the upcoming magazine. 'It'll be across from a lovely piece on Nick Hancock's new greenhouse...no, I don't think he does live around here anymore but I'm sure he must have fond memories of growing up here. OK, well thanks for considering it anyway and I'll maybe try you again in six months.'

Geraldine wasn't a naturally gifted salesperson, and so the £27,000 OTE that was advertised ended up at about half that. She didn't mind though because she liked where she worked and the atmosphere. The rest of the office girls called her Geraldine to her face and behind her back called her Smellaldine or Sweaty Betty or Stinky Geraldine. And it was certainly true that she did. She smelled of congenital body odour, overly-worn clothes and a house that had at least five too many cats (and a total of seven cats). The body odour was hereditary and was one of two things she had inherited from her late father - the other being three of the aforementioned cats. 'A lot of them were rescue cats when we got them,' she would tell the office girls with an earnest smile.

'I think they need rescuing from you,' would have been a smart if slightly crass response. But that's not what the girls said. Instead, they would wait for Geraldine to turn back to her computer screen and then hold their noses and think 'daft cow' or 'smelly bitch.' The young lad in the office didn't think 'smelly bitch', but he did think 'Who has seven cats?!' And he didn't speak up to defend Geraldine when she left early each day to pick up her mother's prescription and the other girls would gag and laugh and repeat all the naive things Geraldine had said that day.

'I'm so glad these windows open,' Lara would say.

'I'm spending beer money on *Febreeze*,' Mandy, who was their leader, would assert at least twice a week. It always got a laugh because Mandy was their leader.

'Do you think we're mean?' Mandy asked the young lad who didn't want to work there.

'I think she's a sweet lady, but I'm glad the windows are open,' was the best he could manage.

'We're not bad people really,' Jenni declared.

'I don't even think Smellaldine knows we make fun of her,' Ronnie said.

But she did. Geraldine did know. And she would do something about it.

For the staff Christmas outing, the gang decided they really should invite Geraldine to come along, even though they thought she would ruin their fun and would probably drink water and want to sing a hymn at the karaoke bar.

'You never know, she might be an absolute slut after a glass of wine.'

'I hope she is. Better than turning up like a nun, hanging around like a bad smell,' Jenni said.

'She is the bad smell!' Mandy declared from behind the water cooler. The other girls went berserk.

Geraldine did indeed ruin their fun until she left early. At the curry house she just had a plate of chips because she didn't really like foreign food because her mother had never cooked it and she didn't want to have an upset tummy. She had water because she didn't drink alcohol and didn't want to make a fool of herself.

'Oh, go on,' Mandy goaded her. 'God will forgive you for having a few drinks - you only live once!' The table applauded. Geraldine drank water. The long skirt she wore made her look like she'd just finished a shift at a puritan showhome, and her perfume somehow accentuated rather than masked her natural odour.

'Smells like a used nappy full of Indian food', Lara sent to the *Whatsapp* group while they were all sitting waiting for poppadoms.

'Stop giggling, she'll know.'

'She won't.'

But she did. Geraldine did know. And she would do something about it.

Geraldine didn't sing at karaoke. The young lad who didn't want to work there had overheard her singing something vaguely religious while she was making her cup of weak tea once, and he thought she had a very sweet voice. But Geraldine had been told that singing could attract the wrong sort of man, so she said she couldn't sing and opted out of karaoke, gently bobbing her head along as Mandy and Jan sang 'I Wanna Sex You Up'.

Geraldine didn't go to the third bar with them. She said it was getting late and she didn't want her mum to be sat up worrying but Merry Christmas and look after themselves. It was 9:05pm.

The girls and the young lad had a lot more fun after that, and several of them were sick and all of them had hangovers and all of them were still feeling groggy when they heard on Monday morning that Geraldine had been knocked down by a hit-and-run and wasn't alive anymore.

They all sat there looking at each other in shock, and then a week later they all went to her funeral apart from Jenni who just had a lot of stuff to deal with practically at the moment.

The funeral was held in the Primitive Methodist Chapel where Geraldine had been baptised; where she had gone every Sunday for 43 years and helped with the tea and biscuits afterward; where she would have got married if she had ever got married. After the service there was tea and biscuits and some egg sandwiches and unheated sausage rolls, and Jack the gardener played a religious song on the organ which sounded horrendous but a little like the tune the young lad had heard Geraldine singing.

'I hope she didn't know all the things we said about her,' Ronnie said as they stood in the car park having a last fag before heading back to work to sell advertising space in *Staffordshire Quarterly*.

'I'm sure she didn't.'

They didn't make fun of her after that for a whole year. And even then, they would stop abruptly and say, 'You shouldn't talk ill of the dead.'

'I'm sure she doesn't know what we're saying,' said Mandy, the leader.

But she did. Geraldine did know. And she would do something about it.

Ronnie was the first to die. Colon cancer aged 55, they said. It was reported that Jenni died in a tragic paragliding accident while on holiday in the Bahamas. Lara was said to have had a heart attack a week after her retirement party while feeding some ducks in the park.

Mandy was the last to die. She lived to 85 and had forgotten most of the people involved with *Staffordshire Quarterly*. And she had forgotten all about Geraldine and her smell, right up until the morning she died. She had been making a cup of tea and a sandwich and the opened tin of salmon would waft an image of Geraldine into her mind and she would start to cry, and her body would feel heavy and she would cry for a good while and then her head would feel lighter. Then she would slowly make her way back to her high-backed chair where the lunchtime newsreader was waiting to be the last face she would see on this side of eternity. There were problems in South Korea and the United States was sending troops somewhere and all the sport would be coming up shortly but she was dead by then.

Mandy opened her eyes and was aware that the sun was bright and she was covered in dust and rubble. She was sitting at the foot of a steep incline, whose bareness matured into grassy heather as though it had reached puberty about halfway up. A beautiful man and a beautiful woman were sitting either side of her, and the man was talking to her while the beautiful woman was holding her hand and gently stroking dirt and grime off her face.

'What's happening?' Mandy asked, and she heard in her voice a tremor - although not of fear and not that of quavering old age. Her words, though all of a quiver, were fresh and young. She looked down at her dirt-stained hands and saw the smooth contours unridged by prominent veins.

'Am I alive?' she asked.

'Certainly.'

'Where am I?'

'Where you have desired and chosen to be.'

'I don't know this place. I thought I was...I dreamed I was an old lady.'

'That wasn't a dream. You were an old lady.'

'So...did I...have I died?'

'You did. But in the right way and to the right thing.'

Coming to her senses as one does after a long nap, Mandy looked behind her and saw a vast expanse of sheet rock dully shimmering out for miles ahead of her. Diminutive statues of crouching people were dotted out haphazardly as far as her vision held, and elsewhere, as numerous as the statues, small cairns of stones broke the texture of the ground. Mandy's nostrils were deluged by a smell of rank putrefied flesh. About ten feet away, a small man and a large lady were erecting one of the stone cairns, a dry-stone wall pyramid, the sort of thing you would see on a Sunday walk in the country. 'Sunday? What's a Sunday?' thought Mandy.

'What is that place?' she asked.

'It's known as the Silent Zone.'

'What are the statues for?' But even as she asked the question, she realised her own mistake. They were not statues; they were people, kneeling with hands clenched and faces set like flint. The beautiful man answered her next question before she asked it.

'Mediators.'

'It's like fishing,' added the beautiful lady with a wide smile.

'What are they fishing for?'

'People, obviously. What do you think the odour is? Only humans could make souls smell that bad.'

The fading smell was overwhelming to Mandy, although the beautiful couple didn't seem to be affected by it. It seemed to be oozing malignantly from the cracks in the stone cairn nearby.

Mandy had lots of questions, but she realised with each gentle stroke of her hand and each firm word from the beautiful man and each clink of stone being moved and placed upon stone that her questions were mere curiosities, not necessary interrogations. She took a deep breath, and began to speak in that young, fresh voice of hers.

'I'm covered in dust and rubble because…'

'That's it…go on,' said the beautiful man. 'Give it a name, call it out, and then we'll go and have some food and never have to talk about it again.'

'I'm here because I was under the ground…under that pile of stones. I had been there for a long time, and I was rotting. That smell is me…or *was* me. And then I asked to come out. I don't remember how.'

'We always dig where the ground is wet,' replied the beautiful man. Mandy put her fingers to her face and traced the paths where tears had irrigated her arid face and opened up a fissure in her hardened heart. But weren't those tears from a long time ago? From when she used to be old?

'Tears of remorse flow uphill to freedom,' the beautiful man said.

'How could you tell the ground was wet?' Mandy asked.

'Your friend told us,' the beautiful man replied. 'Geraldine.'

'Geraldine? Geral…I don't remember a Geraldi…' Somewhere an old lady opened up a can of salmon and with it a memory and with that an escape route. 'Yes…Geraldine. She died. I was horrible to her.'

'She's been here mediating for you for what would you call forty five years.'

'Forty five years?'

Mandy looked out at that place where the stone cairns lay as testaments to the death of Death, and the steep bank where the shale and flint gave way to bouncy heather. She wanted to climb that bank, 'upwards to freedom' the beautiful man had said.

'Forty five years? With the hard ground and the putrefied air?'

'Oh,' said the beautiful lady with a shrug, 'Well, yes, but I didn't really mind the smell, old friend.'

nineteen

A NIGHT IN HEBDEN BRIDGE

(An extract from *The Wayfarer*)

I was blister- and injury-free and my walking poles had been quite good entertainment as twirling batons, but the drawn-out tedium of walking all day in isolation had left me bored# as I made my steady descent into the Calder Valley. The valley acts as a natural escalator, conveying you through various department store-style floors of habitat: from windswept moorland, past cattle-studded farm pastures, down through sweet-smelling groves of oak and birch, and finally to the cafe-strewn waterway at ground level. I landed alongside the Rochdale Canal, opened up *Google Maps* (shielding my phone from a fresh influx of raindrops) and triangulated my position in relation to my accommodation.

The route took me strolling back along the canal and through the gentrified streets. A former textile town (previously a jungle of chimneys held together by its own grime), Hebden Bridge had been upcycled and re-upholstered into a hive of hippyfied fashion and liberal values, with a hint of the dark arts lurking somewhere beyond the wall of sleep. It felt otherworldly, but maybe I just hadn't seen civilization for three days.

'Expect nothing and you'll always be surprised,' Daniel Defoe wrote. Today was the only time I was to stay at a private residence (a back-to-back terrace newly listed on *Air BnB*) rather than a bespoke walker's inn. My hosts were an Austrian couple in early retirement named Werner and Ingrid, and Werner had come across as very enthusiastic in his correspondence. I arrived at 4:30pm, the hour when the soul sinks lowest, and, after ringing, hammering and wailing 'Pleeeeaaaasssseee', I waited outside in the now pouring rain for an hour because they must both be out. As it transpired, only Werner had been out. Ingrid was in the whole time but suffers from depression so doesn't answer the door unless she feels like it. On this occasion, she didn't.

Werner finally arrived and opened up, leading me through into what can best (perhaps only) be described as an Aladdin's cave of psychedelic erotica. Ingrid was apparently a very talented but quite rude artist, and had adorned practically every surface and wall with quasi-spiritual and fully-porno paintings and sculptures, including one just above the *Aga* of my two hosts wearing coy smiles when underwear would have worked better to my taste. I was handed a chai tea and engaged in avid conversation by Werner, while never really being able to take my focus off the acrylic of his liberated genitals perennially in my eyeline. Seemingly an acolyte of the realist school of art, Ingrid had not *ahem* been kind to Werner in the scale of her work - a creative move I would have applauded had my hands not been otherwise engaged in forcibly detaching my retinas.

'That's certainly me!' Werner chuckled shamelessly.

No wonder she's depressed, Alan whispered. I told him not to be crass and took another long, studious sip of chai, closing my eyes to fully appreciate the delicate oriental flavours and also to block out the baying mob of willies nestled in my peripheral vision.

I should have just left at that point. 'It is never too late to be wise,' Daniel Defoe wrote in Robinson Crusoe. I really could have done with reading about Daniel Defoe before I started walking the Pennine Way - he seems like my sort of guy.

'Would you like' to have a bath?' Werner enquired of me after a blessedly short and completely harrowing tour of the house.

'Yes please, but on my own if possible,' were my exact words. If live conversations had an edit button, I'd almost certainly look to redact the 'if possible' part on the second run.

'Ja, that's possible,' Werner replied. Not preferable, notice - but possible.

'How long will you be?' he asked with slight consternation.

'Erm, I don't know, I was hoping to have a long soak.'

'It's just that we only have one toilet in the house and it's in the bathroom. What if I need to do a wee?'

'Maybe you should go and do a wee now?' I suggested, really starting to project manage this crisis.

Werner went for a wee while I stood outside with my towel. He was out quickly enough.

'Hang on, let me just check with Ingrid - she's upstairs painting...Ingrid?!...Ingrid?!' Werner called up to the attic room.

'...Ja, wass?'

'Andy chooses to have a bath. Do you need to do a wee first?' There was a delay while Ingrid divided her daily fluids intake by the average length in minutes of a domestic soak, timesing that by the urgency of whatever bottom she was painting.

'...Ja, Ok, I come and have a wee too.'

'Ingrid comes to have a wee too,' Werner informed me.

'Yep, I got that.'

Ingrid came down the stairs, ghosted past me into the bathroom to have a wee and, surely contravening all unwritten lore of hospitality, also a poo. Six minutes later and Werner and I were still standing there.

'I think she may be taking a poo as well,' Sherlock Werner confided. 'I'll just check...Ingrid...Ingrid...are you taking a poo too?'

Less of a pause this time.

'Ja, sicher.'

'She's taking a poo, too,' Werner confirmed.

'Thank you.'

I was changing my mind about this bath. On reflection, that hour standing out in the pouring rain had got me pretty clean. More than that, it had been a magical time, a golden age of innocence.

Over a late-night potion of homemade kefir (which Werner brought into my unlockable room while I was trying to Facetime my girls and stayed there until I hung up) he laid out his plans for breakfast the following morning.

'Usually, we eat around 9:30am, a breakfast of oatmeal and melon tea. How does that sound?' His ingratiating smile suggested he was expecting me to gush gratitude.

*Is he ******* joking*, Alan asked from the windowsill.

'Do you have any hash browns?' I asked.

'No.'

I had found myself in a culinary cul-de-sac, and there was no way to reverse.

'Oatmeal and melon tea sounds…just like breakfast to me.'

'Ah, wunderbar, excellent.'

It was 10pm and I was exhausted. A perfect time for Werner to dive headlong into a no-context diatribe about vaccinations, casually admonishing me as he did so for getting my Covid jab. 'Don't have your second one, whatever you do - you'll be dead in three years.'

I glanced around at the swirling pantheon of aggressive nudes, recollected the odious bath from earlier in the evening, and sloshed some of the sour yoghurt bacteria around in my mouth.

'…Good,' I said. 'I want to be.'

twenty

THE SHARPSHOOTER

I met Mr. Nathaniel Dorset in the September of 1886. It was the fall, and the heat of the summer was still hanging in the air, hanging like a condemned man; and the winter making its slow, inexorable long march to take up its battle line.

I came upon the aforementioned gentleman on the streets of Lafayette, Indiana. I was there on account of work, or rather my urgent need for it, having hopped and bolted from job to job like a startled buck, always with an unfortunate and premature ending: either my employer died in an untimely and selfish manner, or he had no further need of me, or on occasions found my work to be below the standard one might set. I feel no shame in saying that— some gentlemen are blessed by the Almighty with gifts as numerous as cherry blossoms, which see them sail unabated through any of life's challenges. For my part, my divine bequeathings are narrow, putting me in mind of a sharp leaden-tipped pencil, lethal for writing but helpless when jabbed repeatedly against masonry. But needs must, and I must needed a job, and there you find me on that warm orange morning.

I had read in a local dispatch that the Lafayette undertaker, a man by the name of Briggs, was on the lookout for manly hands to help with the unfortunate pressing need for coffin makers, on account of a resurgence in cholera deaths. However, upon presenting myself before Mr. Briggs, I was told that he had more than enough men to aid him in his grim but worthy endeavors;

but, said he, with the cholera still advancing, might I return in a week and see who was still alive on the premises. I did not appreciate the dark humor of his words, and so it was with disconsolation that I found a friend in a bottle of whiskey, and another friend in the shape of Mr. Nathaniel Dorset. I espied him from my dugout position at the Silver Dollar saloon, sitting statuesque in its wide window, swilling some liquid around in his glass without ever seeming to take even a sip, a look on his face of the gravest and deepest ennui, and with the finest pair of brown leather boots that I had seen in my thirty nine years on God's green earth. After some time had passed in this manner, me gazing, him sitting and swilling, and with no particular plans for the rest of my day, I chanced to approach him and to enquire as to the origins of his apparent black mood.

"Sir, I am on the lookout," he told me, with a resolve that in no way matched his expression, and with an accent that betrayed him as an Englishman, and one from the higher ranks of that realm. He was not, by modern standards, a handsome man: his facial features were of splendid proportions, if one were looking at a horse; but his countenance was mapped out with such singular pain and woe that I chanced to pry a little further into his meaning.

"What is that for which you are looking, sir?"

"I am in search of a killer," he said, not shifting his gaze from the outside street for even a second.

"You are with the Pinkerton agency?" I enquired candidly, not wishing to seem impertinent. His eye twitched a little with impatience.

"I wish to employ a killer," he clarified. "A man who can kill without a moment's thought."

Had I not been observing this man for a good while, I would have written him down as a drunk, besotted with the demons of liquor. But I have seen drunkards and known too many, and they do not take their time over their drink; they race through it, chase after it, before whatever pain they are retreating from can overtake them.

"What method of employment would this killer be required to undertake, sir?" I asked, fearing that I may incite this man's rage with my continual temerity, but struck with a fascination as to the origin of the gentleman's cause.

"I need him to kill, sir, obviously. A killer is required to kill a killer."

"That has the ring of a riddle, sir," I said, to which his mouth twitched at the corner, perhaps with low mirth, perhaps not. I would have left the man to his riddle and to his hawkish gazing, had it not been for two reasons: the first being my need for employment of any kind; and the second being my precise qualification as the sort of man for which he was looking. I took a seat opposite him, and gave the table a kind of gaveling with my knuckles so as to have his attention for my presentation.

"If I may introduce myself, sir, my name is Zechariah J. Maddison and I am a former soldier."

The man scoffed. "Every man above the age of thirty five in this establishment is a former soldier," he replied, not without merit.

"Forgive me sir," I said in turn, "I had not quite finished. I served in the 2nd United States Sharpshooters under Colonel Berdan."

"Pah! Wasn't that regiment annihilated?" came the man's reply.

"Well, sir, we lost a lot of men, that is the truth of it; but I was not one of them, on account of my ability to shoot pretty straight and pretty accurate, without thought one might say."

At this, finally the man cocked his head to look at me, and I saw in his saucer gray eyes the full weight of grief that he was carrying in his soul. His body and his voice were that belonging to a statesman maybe, but in those deep eyes I saw the fear of a small boy.

"So you are a…killer, sir?" he asked, laying emphasis on every word.

"To my transient glory and endless shame, I am indeed…sir." And there was no lie in that. In my darker moments, I hasten to the belief that the one thing in life at which I have shown extraordinary capacity is the taking of the life of others.

"See there?" the gentleman asked, pointing a long, elegant finger out towards the street. "Notice that high cross on the church steeple?"

"Yes, sir, I see it."

"Could you hit that from here?"

"…Indeed I could sir, with the right weapon. I would need a Sharps rifle."

"Would you, though?" he continued in a very grave tone. I hesitated, anxious that there might be a philosophical underpinning to his question. I began to respond, but was stopped in my tracks.

"If it was a man, and I ordered you to fire upon that man, would you do it?"

It would paint me in a brighter light, and would therefore be preferable to me, if I could inform you that I hesitated in my response; but I cannot tell you that.

"Yes, sir, I would. I would fire, and you would see a church without a steeple."

My new friend seemed to freeze; not with fear, but rather with the dry focus of a man who unexpectedly has gained the upper hand in a fight, and wants to savor it a while.

"You have family?" he asked, after a good minute had elapsed.

"No, sir, I do not. My wife died coming up on three years ago. I have no children."

"You have a place of work, then?"

"No, sir. I came here today following the scent of employment, but that trail has gone cold."

He coughed, clearing both his throat and his thoughts simultaneously.

"Well then, Mr. Maddison, I wish to employ you. I can offer you $100 per week."

At this pronouncement, my heart began to move with great gaiety around my chest, as though it wanted to pop right out and drink to the gentleman's health.

"And how many weeks would that be for, may I ask?"

"Until it's done," he replied.

"I see. And when would we begin? How will I meet you?"

"It begins now; indeed, it has already begun. You own a rifle?"

"I own one sir, sure enough, but I do not have it in my possession."

"Then our first stop will be to the gunsmith."

And so, in the blink of an eye and the drink of a rye, it began.

In grand total, I spent fourteen days and nights with Mr. Nathaniel Dorset, and each one was like taking a step farther down a rocky path towards an unseen cove, unsure whether one would find at the bottom a rock pool of deep redemptive blue, or simply a fatal bed of jagged rocks. To this day, many summers on and in a distant region, I cannot do much more than sketch in pencil outline the man whose life I may have saved. I believe there was a rich fertility to his character, albeit his persona was that of an overgrown garden, covered over with the moss of time and with the lichen of grief. However, I hasten to say that he was, without hesitation or shadow of doubt, a man whose honor plumbed deeper even than his pain, and maybe that is the truest art a man can paint. In this existence that some people have taken to calling "life", encountering a man who promises to cross your palm with silver is liable to send quivers along the boundary line of one's credulity. The human race churns out con-artists and snake oil salesmen as though there exists in some hidden realm a kind of diabolical West Point. But Nathaniel Dorset was a man of his word. By sundown on the opening day of our acquaintance, I had been yoked with a spangly new rifle, two cartridge boxes of high-velocity ammunition, the loan of a Missouri Fox Trotter for the duration, and a barrel's load of canned provisions and salted meats that filled not only my modest knapsack, but also my heart and my belly.

"You may eat whatever you wish, whenever you wish," Mr. Dorset told me with commanding softness. "You look like you need more than one good meal, and I am determined to help you to that end."

I replied that I was not in the custom of hearty feasting, but that it was a vice whose acquaintance I was more than willing to make.

Aside from his blunt cajoling that I distend my stomach, which had shaped itself through years of sparsity into the appearance of a washboard, Mr. Dorset was singularly sparing with his words those first couple days. I have encountered Englishmen since that time, and have found them to be as reckless with their words as they are meticulous with their dress, grapeshotting their opinions into polite company in the faint hope that one may strike home. But Mr. Dorset never wasted his words, in the same way that a rifleman never wastes a bullet, and I appreciated that very much.

We camped that night on a bluff overlooking a creek whose name I did not know and do not know still, although it is little brother to the Wabash. Mr. Dorset sat by the amber light of the crackling fire, saying little; his long fancy coat, faded by a climate which shows no favoritism to social hierarchy, tight around his shoulders; his extraordinary brown leather boots gleaming like polished bronze in the reflected firelight. I never once saw him slouch; he always sat upright like a rake, alert and attentive, as though his instincts had sensed beyond the campline some unseen foe or hidden danger. I had asked him as we rode our horses out of Lafayette, him riding with the ease and formality of a royal procession, I swaying around like bulrushes in a storm—for I am not a natural horseman—whether he knew the precise whereabouts of the man whom we were stalking.

"Indeed, Mr. Maddison," he replied, "I know where we are headed. Only the Creator may know at what exact place and which precise moment a man's life will be snuffed out, but I have a shrewd idea as to the fellow's whereabouts."

"And may I inquire as to why you wish to kill this man?" I asked, looking down into my plate of bean stew.

"You may ask, but I may beg your pardon and refuse the license. I will not tell you—not yet."

"Why, I feel as though I were in a mystery novel, sir."

"There is no mystery, Mr. Maddison; there is only forbearance."

Whilst my friend remained guarded over his own plans and origins, he nevertheless sucked my own life story out like a snakebite. The following day, as we stitched a narrow path between corn fields, the farm hands hot at their work looking up at us with the curiosity with which one might stare at a talking bison, Mr. Dorset pressed me hard on my battle experience, and, I suspect, my battle readiness; for though I had offered my credentials on the occasion of our first meeting, I could very naturally have been spinning yarn, a desperate man rolling deadly dice for a bag of coins.

"When did you first shoot a man?" he asked around noon from the shadow of a walnut tree. We had ridden all morning, and my buttocks were threatening to secede from the rest of my body.

"I am assuming you mean during the War, sir?"

"It is not a complicated question, Mr. Maddison," he said blithely. At this, he took a bite of a peach and scratched his thinning pecan-colored hair, which had become black with sweat and tousled beneath his faded blue bowler.

'Well, sir,' I replied, 'in that case I cannot fail to give you an uncomplicated answer. I was sixteen years old, and I took the finger off a man whom I had found touching my sister in a barn."

Mr. Dorset was not anticipating this statement, and he peered a calculating look at me from under his brow. His mouth twitched open and shut a couple times like a beached fish, but his rod-like English rectitude prevented him from asking the question which I wager was somewhere behind his lips.

"I was ashamed of myself for that," I confided, scratching my own cap–which was as shapeless as a feedbag–not wishing to drag an uncomfortable silence in our wake.

"You were defending a loved one, though, were you not?"

"Yessir, I was, and it is not that for which I was ashamed."

"For what then?" he asked, turning the piece of fruit over in his hand like a broken world.

"Well," I said, with rising humility, "I had meant to snap the fella's hand clean off at the wrist, but I had only recently risen from slumber, and my aim was still washing its face and drinking its morning coffee."

Mr. Dorset did not laugh at this, but he patted his thigh twice with a flat, gentlemanly hand–I believe as some acknowledgement of the humor, although I cannot be sure, for I never once heard him laugh. Only once, for that matter, did I see him smile, but it was not there under that walnut tree.

"Did you find yourself in trouble after that occurrence'" Mr. Dorset asked, his peach very much a beaten man in their struggle for survival.

"That, sir, is indeed a more complicated answer. My Pa smothered me with the only embrace I ever recall receiving from him, while my Ma took her best flour off of the shelf and baked me the finest blueberry cake I have tasted before or afterwards; but they told me that I must give my full attention to leaving town, and be devilish quick about it. My brother took me by cart to Lansing, my sister blubbering her thanks and sorrow the whole way, and I enlisted in the United States Army. Within two swishes of a rabbit's tail, it seemed to me, I was at the Camp of Instruction in Washington, firing round after round into gray-coated scarecrows.'

**

On the fourth day of our "adventure" we rode into the town of Lebanon, Indiana, a strong outpost of hickory trees acting as sentinels along our approach. We had no lack of provisions still, but we entrusted the horses to a brittle-boned and gold-haired stablehand–I had named mine "California Joe", after a man from my regiment whom I did not like–and took up temporary residence in the first saloon that we arrived at, for there were many. Mr. Dorset beckoned a bottle of bourbon off of the shelf and handed it to me; then he dug himself in at the window seat and played poker with his thoughts, while I played poker with a pair of charming skullduggers, who took my money, and would have taken my knapsack had I not kept my Sharps rifle slung across my shoulder the whole time. When my money was mostly gone, the whiskey bottle half-empty like an hourglass, and while I was juggling the morality of finding a young lady with whom I might take a short nap and some horizontal refreshments, my attention was drawn by a sudden blur coming from the window enclave. Mr. Dorset had bolted from his seat and crashed through the saloon door, with such intrepidity that I wondered if he might perhaps be on fire. A commotion was coming from the outside street–the shrieks of a woman and the rasping tone of a man. Decidedly less steady on my legs than I had been earlier, I hastened to the opening, a wobbling steam locomotive which has been derailed on account of rotten sleepers. I gained the street in time to see Mr. Dorset grab the hair of the rasping toned-man, who in his turn had a hold of the shrieking woman's ponytail. Mr. Dorset set off down the street as though on some evening constitutional associated with his class, his prey near horizontal and kicking dust in a futile attempt to halt the proceedings. Finding a suitable spot in the middle of the blessedly empty street, Mr. Dorset flung the man to the ground like a pelleted squirrel, and stood over him.

"How dare you, sir!" he shouted, misplacing his composure for a second, then finding it once more. "How dare you mistreat a woman in this way."

The floored man rolled backwards and rose swiftly to his feet; then he lunged at Mr. Dorset with a wild fist–to little avail. Mr. Dorset, with lightning speed and high disdain for any personal injury, stepped briskly to one side and slammed his own gentleman's fist into the back of the local's head–at which, the local man, his face leading from the front, crashed down into the dirt like the final kill at a turkey shoot.

"How dare you, sir," he said again, in a much quieter voice; then he turned his back, and concluded his afternoon stroll by walking over to the woman in question, who sat cowering across from the saloon. Neither I, nor the card-sharking skullduggers who had joined me to watch the bout, heard what was said after that. My rifle, which by instinct I had unslung from my shoulder and began to prime, was not needed on this day, and I believe that was a mercy. What may also have been a mercy was that I would not be taking my nap.

"That was rightly a noble thing you did back in Lebanon," I told my friend that evening. We were camped in the middle of some cedar thickets, hard up against a railway embankment; Mr. Dorset atop a fallen tree, statuesque in his triumphant regality. He laid down his plate–on which, as I remember, was a concoction of canned salmon and baked beans–and held me in his sights for a good, long while with those ghostly gray eyes.

"My wife was murdered by a man such as that, Mr. Maddison," he said, his voice and eyes holding steady; his thoughts, perhaps, driving westward to an untold degree, harnessed by the mystic chords of memory. Whatever mystery had been held back until that moment was now revealed.

"I am earnestly sorry to hear that, sir"' I replied, at which he nodded. "I believe I now know who it is that we are hunting. Am I mistaken?"

"You are not, sir," he said.

I have known more silent men in my time than I have known womanly caresses; men for whom the opening of their souls to a public audience would require prolonged and gruesome torture, the cracking of a clam shell under a rock hammer. But that evening, under a Midwestern sky, when Mr. Nathaniel Dorset began his advance of self-disclosure, it was more like the slow opening of an inner door to a trusted companion. He told me of his early life in the county of Middlesex; of his father's business in the textile industry, and how he had inherited that cumbersome yoke; of how the desire for expansion and empire had led him to bring his young wife–with her sharp Irish face and sapphire eyes– across that wide expanse of water to the New World; of how she never wanted that. I listened well, eyes on the fire, fingering my cap; noticing the mosaics of mud which had bespattered it since we left Lafayette. Then, quite abruptly, Mr. Dorset broke off–

"I have his coat."

"Whose coat, sir?" I asked.

"The coat of the man who murdered my wife." At this, he unfurled his bedroll and drew out a long, gray coat. Even in the meager light afforded by the dying fire, I could see that it belonged to a man who bathed in opulence, and one much larger than my friend.

"A gentleman like you, sir?"

"No! No, he was no gentleman." Once again, Mr. Dorset struggled momentarily to bridle his composure in the presence of his alacrity.

"It seems unjust that one so cruel should have been blessed with such riches," I said.

"Man looketh on the outward appearance, but the Lord looketh on the heart," he replied, quoting, I must assume, a text from the Scriptures. Then, his emotional tranquility re-established, Mr. Dorset once again changed course with alarming calmness.

"How does it make one feel to kill a man in cold blood, Mr. Maddison?"

"I beg your pardon, sir? I don't see the connection.'"

"My apologies. You mustn't answer if you would rather not. I am not a military man, and it is a question which has often gained access to my thoughts: what does it to do a man to kill in cold blood?"

My thoughts on that subject are as thick as fleas on horseshit, and I waited a moment to see which of them would settle.

"Well, sir," I began, "for me that was quite simple. I killed in cold blood on account of wanting to keep my own blood warm."

My friend exhaled—not a laugh, nor a scoff; rather an involuntary escape of air.

"So simply an primal act of self-preservation—is that it?"

"No, sir, I do not believe that is fully it. I took pleasure from it. It was my gift; that small pouch of my being in which I stored my honorable manhood. Some men with whom I fought took up arms to save the Union; some to free the negroes. For my part, I fought and fired, and reloaded and fired again, because that was how I was able to leave my mark on the world. A man who builds a barn leaves a legacy; a man who builds a town, an even greater one."

"And a man who shoots a man who builds a town—an even greater one?"

"Oh, but sir, it does not profit a man to think too deeply about the autobiography of the fella he has felled. They were strangers, all of them. And I never actually saw them: whenever I fired, I only ever saw that man's wrist, the one that so stole from my sister her childhood. As a rifleman, you aim small; you shoot for the heart. But always—always—I aimed at that wrist."

I have no desire to rewrite history at this juncture; it is important that I lay down bare facts as far as I am able. A finer and more romantical writer may here suggest that Mr. Dorset was deeply moved by my story, and that under that black sky and reflected from the light of the fire, I witnessed tears spring in his eyes. Well, I may well have done, but I cannot be certain. I have downed a bull elk at dusk from two hundred meters, but even the eyes of a sharpshooter can not see that deep into a man's heart.

"And that is why, Mr. Dorset,' I rejoined, "you must refrain from telling me anything about this man I am to shoot–do you understand? Not even about his coat. Just let me see the wrist."

"But you can at least shoot a man in a gray coat?" he asked, in a strangely pastoral tone. I could not help but chuckle at this, and drinking down the final remnants of the bottle of bourbon, I raised it in salute.

"I can that, sir. I surely can."

He touched the rim of his bowler cap by way of acknowledgement, and nodded.

"Good night, then, Mr. Maddison."

"Good night, Mr. Dorset."

**

We continued south in a dog's leg fashion. Through Indianapolis, that prosperous pork-packing city, where we spent a pleasant night in a hotel and ate mighty well; then down towards Louisville. We encountered no trouble, made no friends; we neither kicked up pace like bounty hunters, nor moved with stealth like a stalking predator: we rode, stopped, ate, rested, rode on. Towns became farmland and back again. The sun, raw and unpeeled, warmed our backs during the day; the moon hosted our suppertime soirees. We would light up our pipes and sit in silence smoking them, huddling for quiet comfort beneath their blanket of embers. Mr. Dorset spoke little those next few days, though I surmise now, later, that that was intentional. Down wide turnpikes and lonely paths we traveled–though every path is lonely when you have lost someone; when each step takes you farther away from the last time you saw them.

On the thirteenth day, late in the afternoon, we crossed the Driftwood River east of Jonesville, and entered a land of meadows and creeks. The rising smoke from a place named Uniontown was visible over the horizon, with low blue mountains to the south-west, silver-tipped in the waning glory of the day. Here, Mr. Dorset unsaddled himself and tugged at the canvas tent stowed on his horse. The air was humid and the ground wet, and I said that I still had some miles in me yet, if Mr. Dorset wished to go farther before making camp.

"That won't be necessary, Mr. Maddison," he said, "for we are nearly there. Tomorrow, all being well, we shall carry out our task.'

The night before battle it was, then. "The bottom was out of the tub", as I recall one company private would say, by habit, once the potential for avoiding a skirmish had been plucked out by the root. I have seen too many nights before battle, and mercifully I have lived to see the nights after them as well, be that as a result of dumb luck or simply the Devil having run out of bullets. Never have I gone to sleep knowing the plan, either divine or military, for the following day; but, in this case, as second-in-command, I decided to risk trial for insubordination by enquiring after the strategy.

"In the event that the man we are seeking is not where you expect to find him, sir—what shall we do?"

"We shall keep looking, Mr. Maddison. We shall seek him until I am poor and you are rich."

"I see. And in the event that we do find him…"

"In that case, I shall flush him out from his hole in the ground, and you, from your vantage point, will do what I have paid you to do."

Mr. Dorset's words were as sharp and as straight as a finely fletched arrow.

"In that case, sir," I said, "I will need to borrow that fancy jacket."

I walked for ten minutes and found a copse of dense white oaks, from whose leader I hung the gray coat. Then I paced back one hundred yards, settling myself in a crouch among the long grass. I took a bullet from the cartridge box, kissed it, nested my rifle against my shoulder, the muscles in my upper back bringing themselves to order, and fired–and missed. A hunk of bark sliced off the tree and lay ashen in the undergrowth, and I cursed accordingly. I rubbed my shoulder blades, rusty from too much peacetime; ran my hand along the barrel of the rifle; breathed in the homely smell of metal and oil and wood grain–remembering. Fixing my gaze on the gallows jacket, I pictured above its neck the face of Jonah Cassidy; pictured in my mind–but not for too long– the sight of him kneading his hand beneath the skirts of my sister, deaf or dumb to her appeals for cessation. Taking a second cartridge, I kissed it twice, loaded it, steadied my breathing–and fired. This time I put a hole right through the left epaulet, just above the heart. Rising, I found another spot farther back and to the side–and sent a bullet straight into the ribcage. Farther back still, and a dull thud in the tree sounded where the man's head would have been–but would not have been any longer. Finally, up on my feet, moving and circling, changing the angle of approach, I sent three more envoys of hissing lead whipping towards that gray coat. They all hit; not all fatally, but no man would be rising early for church after that. With the speaking trump of fame ringing in my ears, I sighted a rabbit scurrying across a far treeline–but a rifle can still bite hard at that distance, and I ensured that he scurried not much farther.

I strolled back to the pair of tents, with the gray coat slung, pheasant-like, over my shoulder; the rabbit dangling by the ears from my other hand. Mr. Dorset, who had been leaning against his horse's saddle, writing what I know now was a letter, looked up at my return and saw me smile.

"How is the coat?" he asked.

"Well, sir," I replied, "it is still right fancy, only there is not as much of it. I fear its owner may not thank us for the state in which it is returned to him."

Mr. Dorset looked at me, wrinkled his brow, and returned to his despatches.

I lit a fire, and set to skinning the rabbit for its part in the nightly feast. I was a man of singular confidence: the campaign was nearing its end; we had food and we had a plan, and I had my rifle–what more can a soldier ask? A soldier does not seek clarification on the wisdom or motive of a battle, and so I did not enquire as to the state of mind or state of courage of Mr. Dorset. I ate my rabbit, washed it down with whiskey, cleaned my weapon, lay in the long grass, and watched my friend polish those incredible leather boots of his. A gentleman must always look smart for war, so they say.

"Are you a praying man, Mr. Maddison?" Mr. Dorset asked me not long before bedtime. The sky had turned decisively from Confederate gray to Union blue, and finally to Prussian black.

"Well, sir, I talk to the sky a lot," I replied.

"Indeed."

"Whether that counts as praying, only the One being prayed to can decide that, perhaps. In all truth, I have seen many things that point me towards heaven, Mr. Dorset, and more than a few that would point me towards hell; so I cannot always feel confident that the Almighty is winning his conquest for the souls of man."

"Indeed," he said again.

"Yes, sir, indeed."

"Say a prayer tonight, Mr. Maddison."

"In what direction, sir?"

"Upwards. And in the direction of Justice. Let us aid the Almighty in his conquest, shall we?"

"Amen to that, sir."

That night, as I had done before the Battle of Antietam, I slept like a newborn foal.

**

For fourteen days, Mr. Nathaniel Dorset had been carrying his sadness around like a bucket of water; but on the following morning–my final morning in his noble company–he seemed rather feather-light, his hopes of revenge–of redemption, maybe– covered in morning dew. A storm was heading for the mountains, the clouds hanging in the sky like a visible curse, but Uniontown was not much more than a mule's kick from our camp, and we reached it by nine in the morning.

"We shall ride straight into town first of all and find the undertaker," my friend said.

"The undertaker, sir? I'm sure I never heard a man invite an undertaker to a fight, no more than he would invite a fox into a henhouse."

Sure enough, we found the undertaker easy enough–a man by the name of Coggins. I waited with the horses, feeding "California Joe" a carrot, while Mr. Dorset strode, with straight-backed resolve, into the establishment. He returned swiftly, his pace picking up to a small degree, and we rode on through the wide streets of the quiet town.

Half a mile out of Uniontown, at a little knot in the road, Mr. Dorset halted as though there were a little knot in his thinking, scratching his head beneath his bowler and darting his eyes to the left and to the right.

"In which direction, sir?" I enquired.

"To the left–this way," Mr. Dorset replied, stretching an elegant sleeve off to where the road dipped into a miniature valley.

"Was the undertaker helpful in confirming the location, sir?"

"He was; he was very accommodating."

"You were fitting the hunted for his coffin, perhaps?"

"I have his coat, Mr. Maddison, do I not?" At this, Mr. Dorset turned his implacable gray eyes upon me, and spoke with grim profundity. "Prime yourself, sir, for now we come to it. Half a mile more. Let justice run down like water, and righteousness like a mighty stream."

We took the final half mile at a near-gallop, slashing off the turnpike into an army of cedars and elms, which cooled the air and chilled the sweat on my back, so that I almost shivered in spite of the heat. And there it was—dug in tight amongst the trees—a stone cottage standing silent and secret, nursed by a steep grassy bank and a chattering stream. It appeared to me like an escaped convict, squat and hidden, keeping its head down from view; indeed, one could have ridden almost over the top of it and not noticed it. A salutary place for a man on the run, and good ground for a brawl. A dirt path led down from where we hitched our horses, and any sound of descent would be covered by the brook.

"You believe the man is in there, sir?" I asked.

"I do, yes," Mr. Dorset replied. "Is this vantage point suitable for you?"

"A surprise attack from high ground, staring down into a narrow gully with no clear escape? It will do just fine, sir."

"That is good," he replied, but I heard in his confident words a tremor of something less than that. From his waistcoat, he now drew a white envelope, sealed and ink-thumbed, and handed it to me.

"Should this end differently to how one expects, I wanted to have your wages to-hand."

"Thank you, sir," I said, with the least enthusiasm with which I have ever received money.

"Quite alright. Thank you for your service." At this, he removed his bowler hat and looked down at the cottage. A brown rat was shuffling around the doorway, unaware of the battlefield on which he was about to find himself.

"I shall head down there now, then," Mr. Dorset said, "and flush him out. Be aware, there is only one doorway. Note that well, Mr. Maddison. If you do not see my face leaving that building–you fire. Is that clear?"

"As clear as an Indiana night, sir," I said, shepherding the tone of my voice, wanting to keep it light.

"Splendid," he replied. "'Shoot for the heart; aim for the wrist'' – was that right?"

"Yes, sir–yes, that's right."

Mr. Dorset wiped the sweat off his palms against his town pants, and offered me his hand.

"Thank you, Zechariah," he said. And then, for the first and the last time, I saw him smile; those deep, sad eyes infected, just for a moment, with something that might have been happiness.

Mr. Dorset, carrying that great gray coat, descended the bank with a slow but resolute formality. I settled on one knee, a gnarled tree root offering some cover–although I did not expect to need any. My rifle was already loaded, but I laid out three bullets, like corpses in a line, on the ground to my right. Sighting my weapon at the single door, a thick slab of oak that looked like a vertical table, I relaxed my breathing–and waited. Mr. Dorset crossed the stream in a single bound and approached the door. He stopped, turned back towards me, and I saw the face of my friend between those iron sights. I watched his shoulders rise and his back straighten, and then he burst in through the door.

Almost instantly, there was a cacophony of noise–of shouts and of crashes. From my vantage point it was impossible, above the noise of nature and water, to hear what was being said, and by whom, but the metallic clashing sounds from within found their way out through holes in the roof, and went off reverberating down the streambed. I was blind and partially deaf to what was happening within those stone walls; at times, the whole dell seemed to grow quiet in fairy tale wonder, but then a clang or a thud would start up again, and I would feel the hairs on the back of my neck stand to attention and my shoulder blades tense. I prayed wordlessly that Mr. Dorset would not be harmed; that he would see his Victory and his Justice.

All of a sudden, the door swung open. A man staggered out, bare foot and tramp-like. His trousers were filthy rags, he wore no undershirt, but he was wearing a gray coat: the gray coat that Mr. Dorset had taken in there–his own coat. Against my instincts, I took my eyes from the sights and looked aghast. I heard no sound coming from inside the open doorway, and my heart plumbed to my stomach; I feared that Nathaniel, after all his woe and strategy, had come off second best. But, maybe not! The man stumbled to his knees, clutching at a hessian sack which had been pulled over his head, and which was impairing his sight–a wild, enchanted scarecrow. A winning horse is not blinkered in that manner, I decided, and, my senses returning to me like rushing water, I sharply returned the rifle to my eyeline, intook my breath–and fired. The bullet struck the scarecrow man right through the heart; blood lashed out in streaks against the stone wall of the cottage, and he fell, face first, into a pool of justice.

In a state of mental and physical exultation, I sprinted drunkenly down the bank, yelling and whipping like a Reb, leapt the babbling stream, and burst into the cottage. Tables had been overturned, there were pots strewn on the floor and shards of glass everywhere, but–but there was no sign of Nathaniel. The cottage had only two rooms, and only one door, and so there was no great search to be carried out.

"Mr. Dorset?" I called out, with consternation; but even as I said those words, my rifleman's eyes fell on a picture by the bedside in the small sleeping quarters. It was a picture of a handsome woman with long black hair, and she was smiling, and she was standing beside a man of considerable girth; a man whom I nevertheless recognised by his eyes. The man was Mr. Nathaniel Dorset. And there, lying neatly and still beside the bed, which looked like it had not been slept in for a good while, was a pair of fine, brown leather boots. A sealed white envelope lay tucked into one of the footholes. Suddenly, a huge weight descended on my body, as though a millstone had been tied round me by some supernatural force. As if in a waking nightmare, I stumbled back outside, over broken glass and broken silence, to the lifeless figure splayed motionless on the ground.

"No, no, no," I said softly, but death cannot be reversed by simple denial, and I knew the future then. Dropping to my knees, I removed the coarse hessian sack from the dead man—and saw the face of my friend.

His great, gray eyes were open, and he was looking up into the fluttering canopy, beyond which the sky was cloudless and sapphire blue—the color of his wife's eyes. His own eyes no longer looked sad, and so I left them open, and let him gaze a little longer up towards heaven. I sat next to him, my head between my legs, my thoughts all mangled, my body heavy as lead.

Before too long—although I cannot say how long, for grief makes of time a concertina—three horses came cantering down the hill at great haste, carrying three men on their backs. One man I recognised as the undertaker; the other two were transparently from the Sheriff's office. They dismounted, and with raised revolvers the two officers came steadily towards me.

"Are you carrying a weapon, mister?" the Sheriff asked me. I told him I was not; I had left my rifle at the top of the bank, and it is still there for all I know.

"Deputy," said the Sheriff, "keep your weapon locked on that man. If he moves, you may shoot him.'

I could not have moved, even if the hounds of hell had been pursuing me.

"We are looking for a white envelope," the undertaker said to the Sheriff, a quiver of uncertainty in his voice.

"Inside," I whispered, as though my voice belonged to someone else.

With some trepidation, the undertaker went inside the cottage, and moments later returned with the envelope, which he handed to the Sheriff. The man opened and read it, and exhaled with heavy consideration. He looked down at Nathaniel's body, and sighed again.

"Well, I'll be damned," the Sheriff said.

"You recognise him, then, sir?" enquired the undertaker.

"Indeed I do," replied the Sheriff. "His name was Nathaniel Dorset. I have only met him once before, on this very spot to be precise, about three years ago, on the day that he killed his wife."

"Lord, have mercy," the undertaker said.

"Deputy, you can lower your weapon," the Sheriff said, with a note of sympathy in his voice. "Whatever crime has been carried out today, the man that you're holding hostage is not the guilty party."

The Sheriff walked slowly over to me, and placed a fatherly hand on my shoulder.

"You are free to go, Mister. I suspect you have had a devilish trick played on you. But I ask that you never return to Uniontown while I am Sheriff. I hope you understand."

I looked up at the Sheriff, the rim of his Stetson turning his face to shadow, and I nodded.

"Oh," he said, handing me the white envelope, "and I think you should read this."

The three men began busily to organize their affairs, and to make arrangements for Nathaniel's body to be taken back to town. I could not watch them–I have never had the constitution for seeing a man's body treated like slaughtered livestock. I sat by the stream, with my back to the stone cottage, and read the letter:

Dear Zechariah,

"I cannot but fail, in words at least, to encapsulate my gratitude for you and for your service. Your sense of duty has made this whole affair far easier than otherwise it might have been, and you must forgive me for my secrecy on the true nature of our quest. I apologise, too, if the man you have killed had become your friend; indeed, I know that killing a stranger is what you have been accustomed to. For my part, I am grateful that it was a friend who carried out this action, and with all authority I absolve you of any guilt which you may feel–today, or at any time in the future.

Zechariah, I loved my wife with all of my heart–and I love her still. I should never have brought her to this land. I was not in my right mind on the day that she died; I had succumbed to a fever, and it played merry hell with my emotions and my judgments. I say this not to free myself of the shame or culpability for what I did, but merely to entreat you not to think too harshly of me. For three years, I have longed to go to her; to take her by the hand and repent of my actions with contrition and woe. "God knows the heart", say the Scriptures, and I hope, perhaps against Hope, that the Divine Judge will see my actions today as a shard of reparation. Either way, I could not continue in this life. I simply desire to depart.

The boots are yours. May the next path they take you down be eminently more pleasurable.

With my warmest, everlasting regards,

Your friend,
Nathaniel

**

Is death a fitting punishment for the taking of a life? Or is life, after the death of a loved one, enough punishment by itself? I do not know; it would take a man considerably more learned than myself to even begin to answer that question. I may only talk for myself, but I can say that my life has changed in two significant ways since that fateful day: firstly, that the Battle of the Stone Cottage was my final engagement as a soldier. Never since have I put my hands on a weapon of any kind–nor shall I. The second change is that I no longer talk to the sky. I may still, by the standards of most respectable folk, be no religious man; but I talk to God, as best as I understand or can picture Him, and I ask, near every day and to this very day, that the desire of my friend–for Grace and Mercy–would have been rightly granted.

I still have those boots–they are on my feet as I write this. They are no longer as shiny or as fine, but they remain a constant reminder of that season of my life; and, wherever I go, I try to tread out a little redemption into the broken surface of this morally uneven earth.

And one other thing, as I finish. I no longer see the wrist of Jonah Cassidy; I no longer use that as a totem for my focus. During moments of high drama, I see only the face of my friend, Mr. Nathaniel Dorset: his gray eyes open and happy; that single smile stretched joyfully–and now, I hope, eternally–across his glorified face.

The End

A NOTE OF APPRECIATION...

Thanks so much for reading this, my sixth published work. I hope you've found something in here that will stick with you.

I am indebted to the friends who read the various drafts of the various stories, and who offered helpful feedback: Tammy G, Liam T, Amy B, Nicola N, Andrew C, Tandy and Dan C, and Lorna F. Legends, the whole bally lot of you!

Special thanks to Francesca Nixon, who acted as proof-reader and sub-editor, and who was very gentle with her words. Superb!

As always, massive love to Mark at McKnight & Bishop publishers. This makes it four books that we've worked on together, and he's usually the best man for the job.

And finally, thanks to Emily Fewtrell, who came up with the title of the book.

If you would like to drop me a line about any of the stories, or if you want me to write something for you, please contact me: andy@andykind.co.uk

That's about it, I think. For now, then, thanks again - and may all your true stories follow a redemptive arc.

All the best,
Andy